HONEY BUNCH HELD ON TO THE THICK MANE.
Honey Bunch : Her First Days on the Farm. Frontispiece—(Page 115)

HONEY BUNCH:
HER FIRST DAYS ON THE FARM

BY

HELEN LOUISE THORNDYKE

AUTHOR OF "HONEY BUNCH: JUST A LITTLE
GIRL," "HONEY BUNCH: HER FIRST
VISIT TO THE CITY," ETC.

ILLUSTRATED BY
WALTER S. ROGERS

NEW YORK
GROSSET & DUNLAP
PUBLISHERS

Made in the United States of America

THE HONEY BUNCH BOOKS

BY HELEN LOUISE THORNDYKE

12mo. Cloth. Illustrated.

HONEY BUNCH: JUST A LITTLE GIRL

HONEY BUNCH: HER FIRST VISIT TO THE CITY

HONEY BUNCH: HER FIRST DAYS ON THE FARM

GROSSET & DUNLAP

Publishers : : New York

CONTENTS

HONEY BUNCH: HER FIRST DAYS ON THE FARM

CHAPTER I

ALMOST SUMMER TIME

"WOULD you care," said Honey Bunch politely, "if I left the door a little open?"

"Close it tight," said Mrs. Miller, turning the wringer as fast as she talked, and that was pretty fast. "Your daddy put the screen door on yesterday because he says it's most time for flies."

"But it's so hot," said Honey Bunch, closing the screen door to please Mrs. Miller. "I thought perhaps we needed air."

Mrs. Miller laughed and stopped turning the wringer. Instead she went over and stirred the clothes in the boiler on the stove. Mrs. Miller was always busy when she was washing.

"The fire makes it hot in here, Honey

1

Bunch," she explained. "But the wire on the door lets in all the air there is to come in. Why don't you stay outdoors and play where it is cool?"

"Mother went down town and I'm lonesome," said Honey Bunch. "Is it summer yet, Mrs. Miller?"

"Dear me, no; and thankful I am it isn't," replied Mrs. Miller, lifting the lid from the boiler. "To-day is extra warm, I'll admit; but we'll have a cool spell before the real hot weather comes. You mark my words."

Then Mrs. Miller turned on the faucet in one of the tubs and the water began to run in so fast and splashily that no one could talk. So Honey Bunch sat down on a chair and whispered to Lady Clare, the beautiful black cat, who opened a yellow eye and seemed to listen.

"You mark my words, summer is coming, Lady Clare," whispered Honey Bunch. "My daddy said so."

"Want to come out in the yard, Honey Bunch?" asked Mrs. Miller, picking up a basket. "I'm going to hang these clothes out now."

Honey Bunch did want to go out into the yard, and so did Lady Clare. They both followed Mrs. Miller up the three little stone steps and out into the yard where some very white clothes fluttered on the line.

"Let me put the pins in?" asked Honey Bunch, who knew all about hanging up clothes; hadn't she helped Mrs. Miller over and over?

"I'll tell you what to do, Honey Bunch," said kind Mrs. Miller. "These clothes are dry and I'll have to take them down. You pick up the pins as I drop 'em on the grass and put every one in this little bag. That will be a big help."

"I'll pick them all up," said Honey Bunch earnestly. "You mark my words, Mrs. Miller."

Mrs. Miller sat down on the lowest step of the back porch and laughed. She laughed easily. Most people laughed, too, when they saw her laughing. Honey Bunch always did.

"You mustn't say everything you hear me say," declared Mrs. Miller, when she had stopped laughing. "Aren't you a funny little girl, Honey Bunch!"

"Am I?" asked Honey Bunch.

"Yes, you are," Mrs. Miller told her, getting up and walking over to the basket which she had left in the middle of the grass. "You're a funny little girl and a dear little girl, and what I should do without you on Tuesdays, I'm sure I don't know."

This was very nice, and Honey Bunch trotted after Mrs. Miller, picking up clothespins as fast as she dropped them and putting them into a little striped bag. When all the dry clothes were taken down, Honey Bunch followed Mrs. Miller up and down while she hung up the clothes she had brought out in the basket. Every time she needed a clothespin, Honey Bunch handed her one. So you can see how nicely they worked together.

"There!" said Mrs. Miller, when the basket was empty. "That finishes everything. I have to clean the laundry before lunch, but I believe I'll sit down and get my breath first."

"Sit down on the step and get it," begged Honey Bunch. "It's so nice outdoors."

It was nice outdoors that morning. The grass was very green and the early flowers nodded gaily from the brown earth and the pear tree at the foot of the yard was a mass of white that smelled as sweet—well, Honey Bunch said it smelled as sweet as a whole bottle of cologne, and it did.

Mrs. Miller sat down on the step again and Honey Bunch sat beside her and Lady Clare came and sat beside Honey Bunch.

"I wish summer would hurry up and come," said Honey Bunch wistfully.

"Seems to me you're in a great hurry," answered Mrs. Miller, fanning herself with her blue and white apron. "You've been asking me for six weeks now when summer was coming."

"Well, I'm going to visit my cousin this summer," explained Honey Bunch. "Not my New York cousins—I went to New York in

the winter. But this cousin you have to go
to see in the summer time."

"Dear me, which cousin can that be?" said
Mrs. Miller, who knew every cousin Honey
Bunch had and who was only pretending.
"Are you going to see your cousin Hazel?"

"I haven't any cousin Hazel!" cried Honey
Bunch.

"Well, then, it must be your cousin Ida,"
said Mrs. Miller, smiling.

"I haven't any cousin Ida!" said Honey
Bunch. "Not a single cousin Ida."

"You'll have to tell me, then," said Mrs.
Miller, making believe to be disappointed.
"I give it up. What cousin are you going to
see this summer?"

Honey Bunch stood up. She was so excited
she almost shouted.

"I'm going to see my cousin Stub!" she
cried. "You know, Mrs. Miller—Stub's real
name is Mary Morton and she lives on a farm.
A real farm and she has a dog!"

"My goodness!" said Mrs. Miller. "What
is the dog's name?"

"I don't know. But Stub will tell me and I'll write it to you on a postal card," promised Honey Bunch. "Stub will tell me how to spell it. Did you ever see a real farm, Mrs. Miller?"

"I lived on one when I was your age," answered Mrs. Miller. " 'Tis a grand place for little girls. But why is a girl with a good name like Mary called such a queer name? Stub! I never heard that before."

"She stubs her toes so much—that's why," said Honey Bunch. "She can't help it, but she does fall down a lot. I don't see why, but she does. She used to cry when she was little, but her daddy made up a verse for her to say when she falls down and now she doesn't cry any more. She says the poetry."

"I wish some one would make up poetry for me to say when I burn my thumb," said Mrs. Miller. "I'm always burning my fingers."

"Uncle Rand can make up poetry about anything," said Honey Bunch. "I'll ask him to make up some for you when you burn your fingers. Shall I?"

"If he isn't too busy," said Mrs. Miller. "But what does Stub say when she falls down, Honey Bunch?"

"I must think," replied Honey Bunch.

When she was a very tiny little girl she had said, "I must sink" when she meant to say, "I must think." But she didn't say that any more. She was five years old and always spoke plainly. Mrs. Miller and Lady Clare waited patiently while she thought of the verse Stub's daddy had taught her to say.

"I know what it is," said Honey Bunch, in a few minutes. "I'll recite it for you."

Honey Bunch stood up again. She could talk better standing up for some reason.

> " 'Stub fell down and hurt her toe,
> Give it a rub and away she'll go.'

"There! Stub says that when she falls down, and then she forgets to cry," said Honey Bunch. "I think it is a nice verse, don't you, Mrs. Miller?"

"Yes, indeed," replied Mrs. Miller. "Much nicer than crying. And where does Stub live, Honey Bunch—as far away as New York?"

"No, not as far away as New York," answered Honey Bunch. "But I don't know just where the farm is. Daddy is going to take us."

"You like to ride on trains, don't you?" said Mrs. Miller. "No wonder you want summer to come so you can go traveling."

Up hopped Honey Bunch again. She had forgotten the most important news of all!

"We're not going in the train!" she cried. "We're going in the automobile! Daddy is going to learn to make it go and we're going to the farm and I'm going to ride in the front seat with him."

"Your mother told me in the winter that Mr. Morton had ordered a car," said Mrs. Miller, her round, red face as excited as Honey Bunch's small pink one. "My land, won't that be fine! Where is this automobile,

Honey Bunch? I'd like to see how you look sitting on the front seat."

"It hasn't come yet," Honey Bunch replied, sitting down more calmly. "It has to come on the train and then Daddy has to learn to run it.   And then—when summer comes—he'll take us to the farm."

"No wonder you want to hurry up the calendar," said Mrs. Miller. "But it won't take your daddy long to learn how to run this car. He knows a heap about them already. I've heard your mother say so."

"Then perhaps we'll go the day after," cried Honey Bunch, dancing up and down on the step.

"The day after what?" asked Mrs. Miller, picking up the clothes' basket and the clothespin bag.

"The day after the automobile comes," said Honey Bunch seriously. "Stub will be expecting us as soon as summer comes, and we ought to hurry."

"Well, I'll have to hurry myself if I'm going to get the laundry cleaned and lunch

started before your mother gets back," said
Mrs. Miller, going down the steps to the laundry. "You stay out and play a while, Honey
Bunch, while I wipe up the floor."

But in a very few minutes Honey Bunch
came quietly down the steps and climbed up
into the chair to watch Mrs. Miller mop the
floor.

"Is anything the matter?" Mrs. Miller
asked her. "You sit there so quiet, Honey
Bunch."

"I came in," said Honey Bunch in a whisper, "because that Norman Clark was in his
yard."

"That's the boy whose folks moved into the
vacant house on the next street, isn't it?" asked
Mrs. Miller, wringing out her mop. "Don't
you like Norman, Honey Bunch? He looks
like a nice little boy."

"Oh, no, he isn't a nice boy," replied Honey
Bunch. "I wouldn't play with him and he
can't come to my next birthday party. He
isn't nice at all!"

"For pity's sake, what is the matter with

him?" asked Mrs. Miller, so surprised that she forgot to go on with her mopping. "Has he done anything mean to you, Honey Bunch?"

Honey Bunch shook her head.

"Well, then, why don't you like him?" repeated Mrs. Miller. "I think he's lonely in this strange neighborhood and you ought to be nice to him."

"He's a bad boy," replied Honey Bunch. "Just as bad as can be. He told me something dreadful."

Mrs. Miller dropped her cake of soap and forgot to pick it up.

"What did he tell you?" she asked. "When did he tell you?"

Honey Bunch climbed down from her chair and ran over to Mrs. Miller. She stood on tiptoe to whisper the dreadful thing Norman Clark had told her.

CHAPTER II

THE CAR COMES

HONEY BUNCH was so little that even when she stood on tiptoe Mrs. Miller had to bend down or she couldn't hear her whisper.

"Norman Clark," whispered Honey Bunch, "went to a party last week. And he told me he—he ate a lady's fingers! Yes, he did. And he likes them!"

Honey Bunch was sure Mrs. Miller would be surprised. She might even be frightened. Honey Bunch had been at first, and now every time she saw Norman Clark she put her hands in her sweater pockets, or if she didn't have her sweater on, she put her hands behind her.

But Mrs. Miller didn't say a word at first. She stared at Honey Bunch. Then she began to laugh. She laughed and laughed and finally she had to sit down in the little rocking chair—Mrs. Miller was so large that you couldn't see the chair at all when she was in it—and wiped her eyes with her apron.

"My dear lamb!" cried Mrs. Miller, "don't you know what lady fingers are? They are little sponge cakes!"

"Are they?" asked Honey Bunch doubtfully. "Why do they call them a lady's fingers then?"

"I think myself it is a silly name," said Mrs. Miller. "But I suppose some one called them that because they are long and narrow. Dear me, I must tell your mother and she will buy some for you and then you won't be thinking poor Norman Clark goes around eating up real ladies' fingers."

Mrs. Miller went on to finish cleaning the laundry and then she went upstairs in the kitchen to get lunch ready. Honey Bunch stayed down, curled up in the chair, thinking about Norman. She wasn't sure yet that he had not eaten a lady's fingers and she meant to keep her own ten pink fingers safely out of his reach till she was sure. Then she thought

about Stub and the farm and the new automobile.

While Honey Bunch is waiting for her
lunch, will be a good time to ask you if you
know her. Do you? If you have read the
first book about her, called "Honey Bunch:
Just a Little Girl," then you know that she was
the kind of friend you would like to have live
next door to you. Any little girl whose daddy
and mother call her "Honey Bunch" because
every time they look at her they are reminded of "sweet things"—as Honey Bunch's
daddy said—is pretty sure to be a lovely small
neighbor. Don't you think so? Of course
this little Honey Bunch had another name, in
fact she had two names beside her last one.
Her real name was Gertrude Marion Morton, and sometimes an invitation to a birthday
party came addressed to her like that.

In this first book about Honey Bunch,
you've been told of the good times she had
with her friends and Lady Clare, the black cat
who wore a white fur collar that looked like
ermine around her neck. Honey Bunch was

busy, too, and she didn't play all the time.
She helped her mother and she fed the birds
and she watched the painters paint the house
and even did some painting herself.

Honey Bunch was a lucky little girl, because she had plenty of cousins. There were
the Turner twins, Bobby and Tess, who lived
in New York; and Stub, the cousin who lived
on a farm; and Julie, another cousin who
lived at the seashore. In the second book
about Honey Bunch (the title of that book is
"Honey Bunch: Her First Visit to the City")
you may read of the visit she and her mother
made to the Turners in New York. Uncle
Paul and Aunt Julia were very glad to see
Honey Bunch and her mother, and Bobby and
Tess were delighted. New York City made
Honey Bunch open her blue eyes wide and
often, but she had a beautiful time and had
some exciting adventures.

Almost as soon as Daddy Morton brought
his little girl and her mother back to Barham,
where they lived, Honey Bunch began to hear
about the visit to the farm. She was eager to

go and visit her cousin Stub, for Stub had
come to her birthday party and had told her
something of the fun that could be found on
a farm.

So that is the reason we find her curled up
in a chair in the laundry, thinking about Stub
and wishing summer would hurry and come.

"Lunch is ready, Honey Bunch!" called
Mrs. Miller. "And your mother's come!"

Honey Bunch ran upstairs. She was very
glad to see her mother, and while they had
lunch together Honey Bunch told her all
about helping Mrs. Miller hang out the
clothes and handing her the clothespins.

"I've been busy, too," said Mrs. Morton,
smiling. "I've been buying dresses for a little
girl to wear this summer."

"Is it time to pack?" asked Honey Bunch.
She bounced around in her chair and nearly
knocked a biscuit off the table. Honey Bunch
was always excited about packing. When she
went to New York she came near packing her
father's birthday cake in the trunk. That
shows how going traveling stirred her up.

"Not yet," replied Mrs. Morton. "Daddy's car hasn't come, you know. Now, dear, if you have finished, run out and play a little while. I want to tell Mrs. Miller about the cleaning this afternoon."

Honey Bunch folded up her napkin. She said "Excuse me" and slipped down from her chair. Then she kissed her mother and went out on the front steps.

"Hello!" called Ida Camp, a little girl about her own age who lived on the same street. "Come over on our porch and let's play farm."

There were several little girls on Ida's porch and they were all eager to play farm. Ever since Honey Bunch had told them she was going to visit Stub, they had had great fun with this play. None of them had ever been on a farm, so if they made mistakes not one of them could scold.

"Let me feed the chickens this time," begged Cora Williams, as Honey Bunch ran up the steps. "Grace always feeds the chickens."

"Yes, it is Cora's turn to feed the chickens," said Honey Bunch.

So Mary and Fannie Graham and Kitty Williams, who was Cora's sister, and Anna Martin and Grace Winters and Ida and Honey Bunch sat down in a row on the steps and Cora pretended she was the mother bird and they were the little ones.

"I'm coming with a nice worm," chirped Cora. "Open your mouths."

All the little girls opened their mouths and chirped:

"I'm hungry! I'm so hungry!"

"What on earth are you doing?" called Ned Camp, coming up the walk and laughing as he saw the seven little mouths wide open and Cora dancing up and down, running from one to the other.

"Cora is feeding the chickens," explained Ned's sister, Ida. "She is the mother chicken."

"But that isn't the way chickens are fed," said Ned, looking so merry and kind that they did not care if he was laughing at them.

Ned was in high school and Ida thought he was the best brother who ever lived. Honey Bunch liked Ned, too. He often brought her catnip for Lady Clare when he went camping where it grew and once he had climbed a tree and rescued the cat when Lady Clare had climbed up so far she was afraid to come down.

"That's the way the mother robin feeds the little robins," said Cora firmly. "I watched the birds that had their nest in our maple tree last summer."

"How do you feed chickens?" asked Honey Bunch.

"Oh, you scatter corn and they come and pick it up themselves," explained Ned. "You'll find out when you visit at the farm, Honey Bunch, and then you can come back and give us all lessons in farming."

Honk! Honk! went an automobile horn so suddenly that every one jumped.

"There's Daddy!" cried Honey Bunch. "Look! The automobile has come!"

Sure enough, a shiny autombile had stopped

at the curb and Mr. Morton sat behind the wheel. He waved to them and beckoned.

"Are there any little girls around here who want to ride around the park and back with me?" he called.

Pellmell down the path ran the children, forgetting the farm game.

"Is it new? Can you drive it? Will you really take us?" seven little voices shouted.

Honey Bunch didn't say anything and Ned opened the door and swung her up on the seat beside her daddy.

"Give me the girl who doesn't try to see how loud she can talk," said Ned. "Shall I ship these other passengers, sir?"

"Well, if they'll ask permission first," answered Mr. Morton, "I'll be very glad to take them. And you, too, Ned. It won't take a minute to ask your mothers, and I'll wait for you."

"My mother won't care," said Grace Winters.

"No little girl rides in my car who doesn't ask Mother first," said Mr. Morton; so Grace ran off to find her mother and was back in a moment so out of breath that she could hardly say:

"She says 'all right.'"

"Can you make it go, Daddy?" asked Honey Bunch, while they were waiting for the others to come.

"Why, yes, dear," said her daddy. "I've driven cars before, you know. I have had my driver's license for a couple of years. But I wanted to get used to this kind of car before I took you and mother on a real trip. This car is a bit different from any I've ever driven. I promise not to spill you out, Honey Bunch."

Honey Bunch laughed. She knew her daddy wouldn't spill her out. He had never tipped her off her sled or dropped her when he was carrying her down the steep stairs.

"Here we are—everybody here?" said Mr. Morton, when all the little girls had come running back and Ned had lifted them into the tonneau, one by one. "Coming, Ned?"

"I'd like to, sir," answered Ned, "but I'm due at baseball practice in fifteen minutes."

"I'll take you out to the grounds. The field is this side of the park, isn't it?" said Mr. Morton. "Hop in."

So Ned stepped in and took Honey Bunch on his lap and away rolled that beautiful shiny car with the spotless new white tires as silently as—as—Honey Bunch tried to think what it reminded her of and at first she couldn't.

"I know!" she said so suddenly that Ned jumped a little. "That's the way Lady Clare goes creeping after a mouse. She runs so still!"

Mr. Morton stopped when they came to the ball field and Ned got out. He played on the high-school ball team.

"Now we'll go through the park and see how near the summer has come to us," said Mr. Morton, smiling at the happy little faces in the back of the car and the happy little face beside him.

"Has it pretty near come?" asked Honey Bunch, when they reached the park.

"Yes, it has," cried Grace Winters. "The leaves are out and the grass is just as green!

'And the yellow flowers are out and the sun is warm. It is summer, isn't it?"

"Almost summer," replied Mr. Morton. "A few more weeks and we'll have June roses."

He drove them through the little park and over the new boulevard home again and each little girl said, "Thank you," and hopped out as he stopped the car before her house. Honey Bunch had a "little extra ride," as she said, because she rode with her daddy to the garage where he kept the car. Then they walked home together.

"Well, dear," he said, as they went in to tell Mother where they had been, "I think next week we'll be off to the farm."

"And I'll feed the chickens," cried Honey Bunch joyfully.

CHAPTER III

THE JOURNEY BEGINS

A FEW days after the new automobile came the deep trunk was brought down from the attic and stood in the upstairs hall. Honey Bunch danced around it, bringing things for her mother to put in it and changing the few toys she was allowed to take three times a day.

"For I might want something else, after I took this," Honey Bunch explained to her daddy.

"That does happen sometimes," he said, laughing. "But you won't need many toys on the farm, dear; you and Stub will be playing outdoors all day long and you'll find the nicest kind of playthings in the fields and in the brook and right in the front yard."

"Mother says not to take but three toys," Honey Bunch explained. "Three to play

with in case it rains or I need to be amused.
Shall I need to be amused, Daddy?"

"You might," he answered. "But look
here, Honey Bunch—do you see this hole?"

They were standing near the trunk while
Mrs. Morton sat on the floor beside it, packing clothes in the tray. Honey Bunch leaned
over and looked down into the trunk. Her
daddy was pointing to a deep hole.

"Do you know what that is for?" asked Mr.
Morton seriously.

Honey Bunch shook her head. She didn't
know.

"Do you know, Mother?" asked Mr. Morton, his eyes twinkling now.

"No, I don't," said Mrs. Morton, folding
up a white dress that belonged to Honey
Bunch. "Unless it is to put Lady Clare in."

"Oh, Mother!" cried Honey Bunch. "You
said Lady Clare was going to live with Mrs.
Miller till we came back."

"So she is, darling," answered Mrs. Morton. "I wanted to tease Daddy, that's all. I
wouldn't pack our beautiful Lady Clare in a

hot, dark trunk. You know I wouldn't do
such a dreadful thing."

So Honey Bunch kissed Mother and said
no, she knew she wouldn't do that.

"Well, if neither one of you can guess what
that hole is for," said Mr. Morton at last, "I
suppose I'll have to tell you."

"Yes, please tell, Daddy," Honey Bunch
begged him. "What is it for?"

"For Stub's present," said Mr. Morton.

"Stub's present?" said Honey Bunch.
"What present?"

"The present you are going to take her,"
replied Mr. Morton. "I think it will just go
into that hole."

Honey Bunch stared at him.

"But I haven't any present to take Stub,"
she said. "Have I, Mother?"

"Oh, but we're going down town now and
buy Stub a present," declared Mr. Morton.
"I have the car outside and I came home especially to invite Mother and you to ride down
town with me."

Mrs. Morton laughed and pulled Honey

Bunch into her lap, on top of the clean dresses.

"How does Daddy expect us to get packed to go away?" she said. "Shall we go down town and buy Stub a present, Honey Bunch, and finish the packing when we come back?"

"Oh, yes, let's!" answered Honey Bunch. "And you tell what to buy, Mother, because you know what Stub likes."

So Mrs. Morton put on her hat and she and Honey Bunch went down and got into the car and rode down town with Daddy Morton. Honey Bunch couldn't think of a single thing that Stub would like them to bring her, but her mother seemed to know what to buy. She found a ring-toss game that was meant to be played outdoors and a little green watering pot with pink posies on it like the one that Honey Bunch had for her garden.

"These will both go in the trunk," said Mrs. Morton to Honey Bunch. "And Daddy has bought a croquet set which he will have sent up by express. Stub's mother wrote me that Stub had lost all the balls of her old set, so I

think she will be glad to have a new one to
play with."

Honey Bunch thought so, too, and all the
way home she was pretending that she and
Stub were playing croquet, Stub with a red
ball and mallet and Honey Bunch herself
with a blue ball and mallet. Blue was Honey
Bunch's favorite color.

The next day the trunk was packed and
locked—the things they had bought for Stub
did go into what Honey Bunch called "the
empty hole" in the trunk and they fitted exactly—and the expressman came and took it
away to go by train.

"We'll have two suitcases to take in the car,
and that is enough," said Mr. Morton. "We
won't carry the trunk with us, as the snail
carries his house on his back."

Mrs. Miller came the day they were to start
for the farm, and she put Lady Clare into a
basket. Honey Bunch hugged her cat and
said good-by and Mrs. Morton hugged Lady
Clare, too, and told Mrs. Miller to take good
care of her.

"And don't let her eat little birds," said
Honey Bunch. "Boiled liver is what she
ought to eat."

Mrs. Miller promised to remember, and she
came down the walk to see them get into the
car. Honey Bunch was so excited she could
not stand still and she bounced around like a
rubber ball.

"Good-by, Honey Bunch," called Ida
Camp from her porch.

"Good-by!" cried Honey Bunch, with a little extra skip. "Good-by! I'm going away
now."

"Good-by, Honey Bunch," called Kitty and
Cora Williams. "Send us post cards."

"If they have them in the country," called
back Honey Bunch, taking two hops this
time. "Good-by!"

"All ready, Honey Bunch?" said her daddy,
who had been busy packing the two suitcases
and the long croquet set in the tonneau. He
had decided to carry the set with them, "so
you may play croquet as soon as you see Stub,
if you want to," he had said to Honey Bunch.

Mrs. Morton was already in the car and
Honey Bunch was lifted in beside her. Then
Mr. Morton went around on the other side
and got in. Mrs. Miller waved her hand, Ida
Camp waved, and Cora and Kitty Williams
waved, too, and the car started.

"Good-by! Good-by!" every one called,
and Honey Bunch saw Mrs. Miller turn and
run into the house.

"She's afraid Lady Clare will get out of the
basket and run and hide," said Honey Bunch
wisely.

And that was just what Mrs. Miller
thought, but she reached the basket before
Lady Clare could climb out. She took the cat
home with her and a very peaceful, pleasant
summer Lady Clare had in her new home.

It was a lovely sunny, summer morning
when Honey Bunch and her daddy and
mother started for "Broad Acres" which was
the name of the farm.

"How far do we go—a hundred miles,
Daddy?" asked Honey Bunch, snuggling
down to be comfortable for a long ride.

"Oh, no, not as far as that," replied her daddy. "About sixty, I think. Did you bring the road maps, Edith?"

"They're in the pocket," said Mrs. Morton, leaning over and patting the leather pocket on the door of the car.

"I don't need them now, but I may later," said Mr. Morton.

"Where does Stub live?" asked Honey Bunch next.

"The name of the town is Elmville," replied Mr. Morton, who was the dearest daddy to answer questions. He liked to answer questions. He said so.

"I suppose you are wondering why Daddy wants a map to tell him where to go," said Mr. Morton, smiling at Honey Bunch. "You see, dear, your mother and I have always gone to visit Broad Acres by train. This is the first time we have ever followed the road. Would you be surprised if we should get lost?"

"You can't get lost, Daddy," said Honey Bunch, chuckling. "Anyway, a policeman will find you, if you do."

But it wasn't long before they were miles away from a policeman. It didn't take long to run through Barham, which was not a large city, and then out on to the boulevard which led them into the country.

"No houses at all," said Honey Bunch, sitting up straight so that she might see everything. "Where do the people live, Mother?"

"They live in houses," answered Mother. "You can't see them, because they are built far apart. See that little trail of smoke in the sky Honey Bunch? That means there is a house there around the turn in the road. Some one is cooking in the kitchen of the house."

"What are they cooking?" Honey Bunch wanted to know.

"Pancakes," said Mr. Morton, turning the car to pass a wide load of hay.

"Lunch," said Mrs. Morton. "Are you getting hungry, Honey Bunch?"

"A little," admitted Honey Bunch. "But shan't we have to wait till we get to Stub's house?"

"Oh, no, indeed!" answered her mother.

"We had an early breakfast, and riding in this nice fresh air makes us hungry, too. Daddy will find us a place to eat pretty soon and we'll stop and have lunch."

Sure enough, in a short time they came to a pretty little town, with beautiful tall trees growing in rows along the streets. The name of this town was Morgan, Daddy said, and he drove the car up before a building that had a large gold sign across the railing of the front porch.

"This is the Morgan hotel," said Honey Bunch's mother, as Mr. Morton stopped the car. "We'll have lunch here."

They went into the house and a pleasant looking woman in a pink and white dress came to meet them.

"Dinner is ready now," she said, smiling. "Would you like to go upstairs first?"

Mrs. Morton said yes, and she and Honey Bunch followed the pink and white dress upstairs. The woman took them into a cool, dark room and said they would find water and soap and towels on the washstand.

"Where's the washstand?" asked Honey
Bunch the moment the door had closed and
the woman had gone downstairs.

Mrs. Morton laughed.

"You never saw one, did you, dear?" she
said. "Well, it isn't much to see. Look over
in the corner and you'll see a washstand."

Honey Bunch looked. She saw a tall white
pitcher and a white bowl and a white dish
with a cake of pink soap on it. These things
were on a table with a pile of clean white
towels.

"I'll pour out the water and then you may
wash your hands," said Mrs. Morton.

She had to help Honey Bunch, because that
small girl was so interested in the washstand
she forgot to wash her face at all and she let
the cake of pink soap melt almost all away
while she tried to find out how deep the water
was in the pitcher.

"There now, we're nice and clean and we'll
go down and find Daddy and have lunch,"
said Mrs. Morton, at last. "Come, dear."

Mr. Morton was waiting for them in the

hall and they went into the dining room together. There were two long tables and several people sitting at each, already eating. Her daddy lifted Honey Bunch into one of the chairs.

"Oh, Daddy!" she whispered, but not so softly that the man across from her couldn't hear, "Daddy, did you see the washstand?"

"IS THAT A LETTER BOX?" ASKED HONEY BUNCH.

Honey Bunch : Her First Days on the Farm.   *Page* 41

CHAPTER IV

RUTH EVANS

THE man seated across the table from the Mortons laughed when he heard Honey Bunch's question. Daddy laughed a little, too, as he sat down.

"When I was a little boy," said the man, his eyes twinkling at Honey Bunch, "I had a washstand in my room and in winter the water used to freeze in the pitcher and I had to pound it with a stick before I could get water enough to wash my face."

"Oh!" said Honey Bunch. "Wasn't it cold? We have warm water that comes out of a faucet in our house."

"To be sure you do," answered the man. "But when your grandma was a little girl she didn't have any faucets in her house."

He had been eating dessert when they went

in and now he had finished. He nodded
good-by and went away.

"Does he live here?" asked Honey Bunch,
as she tasted a baked potato the young waitress
brought her.

"I don't think so," answered Mrs. Morton.
"I imagine he is traveling and just stopped
here for his lunch. But you mustn't talk so
much, Honey Bunch, or we'll never get off.
Drink your milk and don't forget the bread
and butter."

As soon as they had finished their luncheon
Honey Bunch and her daddy and Mother
went back to the car. They drove away down
the shady street and through the town. Morgan wasn't very large, and most of the streets
were short and turned suddenly. The moment they were past the last house, Honey
Bunch made a discovery.

"The sun has begun," she said.

"Goodness, Honey Bunch, are you making
up poetry to tell Uncle Rand?" asked Mrs.
Morton.

"Is that poetry?" questioned Honey Bunch eagerly.

She said it over several times to herself. "The sun has begun, the sun has begun," and finally she decided that it *was* poetry.

"Yes, it must be poetry," agreed Mr. Morton, his eyes on the road. "I never could understand poetry and I don't understand this. What does 'the sun has begun' mean, Honey Bunch?"

"Why, it means," said Honey Bunch, very slowly and carefully so that Daddy should understand, "that—that the sun has begun, Daddy. Just as soon as we left Morgan the trees stopped and the sun began. Don't you see?"

"Now I do," he replied. "The sun did begin to pour down on us, didn't it, dear? It would be nice if we could have a shady road all the way to Elmville, but no one has planted the trees."

Then Honey Bunch asked about the trees—who planted them and why some places had

trees and some didn't and how long it took a
tree to grow and whether her daddy had ever
planted a tree and where was it now?

By the time Mr. Morton had answered all
of these questions they were far out in the
country. Sometimes they saw men working
in the fields, and when they waved to the
speeding car Honey Bunch and her mother
waved back. The sun was hot, but the top
was up and an automobile can always bring
you a breeze, you know, as long as it is going.

"There's a tree!" cried Honey Bunch,
pointing ahead. "There's a tree, Daddy!"

"I'll stop there and take a look at the engine," Mr. Morton said. "You and Mother
may like to take a little walk while I'm tinker-
ing."

The tree was a cherry tree—so Mrs. Morton said—and it grew inside the fence but
spread its green branches far out over the
road. Mr. Morton drove up under it and
stopped the car.

"Is it broken?" asked Honey Bunch anxiously.

"No, indeed," said her daddy cheerfully.
"I want to poke the engine's insides, that's
all. I think I can make it run more
smoothly."

"We'll take a walk down this lane," said
Mrs. Morton. "Come, dear. We won't go
far and Daddy can call us if he finishes before
we get back."

A few steps beyond the cherry tree there
was a lane. Honey Bunch thought it looked
just like a street, except that there were no
houses and no sidewalks and no people.
There was a letter box, though, right at the
corner where the lane joined the road.

"Is that a letter box?" asked Honey Bunch,
when Mother told her what the white tin box
with the little red flag was meant for.

"Surely it is," replied Mrs. Morton.
"When the little flag is up, that means the letter carrier has left a letter."

"It's up now," said Honey Bunch. "Who
is the letter for, Mother?"

"There must be a farmhouse near here,"
answered her mother. "And the letter is

meant for some one who lives in the farmhouse."

"But will the letter man go and tell them
there is a letter?" went on Honey Bunch, so
interested in the mail box she forgot to walk.
"How will they know there is a letter for
them, Mother?"

"Come on the shady side of the path, dear,"
said her mother, "and I'll tell you while we
are walking. In the country, Honey Bunch,
the mail comes only once a day. The postman leaves it in these boxes. Every family
has a tin box like this one. Some one comes
and gets it once a day, too."

"But maybe there isn't a letter for everybody every day," said Honey Bunch. "Sometimes the letter man goes right by our house,
Mother, and doesn't leave us a thing."

"Sometimes he drives right by the country
letter box, too," explained Mrs. Morton.
"But the people who live in the country usually go once a day to their mail boxes, anyway. Most of them take a daily paper, and
that means there will always be something in

the box. Here comes some one for the mail now, I do believe."

Honey Bunch looked. Coming toward them was a little girl, a year or two older than Honey Bunch, perhaps. She wore a brown gingham dress and she had brown eyes and hair and some brown freckles on her little nose.

"Hello!" said Mrs. Morton, smiling, while Honey Bunch and the little girl stared at each other.

"Hello!" said the little girl shyly.

"My little girl and I were talking about the letter box at the end of the lane," said Mrs. Morton. "I told her how the letters are delivered in the country. She is going to visit this summer on a farm, and I am sure she will find letters in just that kind of a box."

"Did you happen to see if the flag was up?" asked the little girl eagerly. "I don't suppose you looked, did you?"

"Yes, we did!" cried Honey Bunch. "The flag was up, wasn't it, Mother? That means there is a letter there! Mother said so!"

"Yes, and that letter is from my aunt," said the little girl. "My cousin Laura is coming to see me next week and now we'll know what train she is coming on."

"We'll turn and go back," said Mrs. Morton. "I think Daddy must be looking for us by this time."

"Did your car break down?" asked the little girl, quite as if she were used to meeting people in her lane whose cars *had* broken down.

"No, nothing's broken, but Honey Bunch and I thought we'd take a little walk while Honey Bunch's daddy tinkered with the engine," explained Mrs. Morton, smiling at the little girl who smiled back and told her own mother afterward that the lady in the tan coat was the "nicest and happiest lady."

"Is that her name—Honey Bunch?" asked the little girl. "My name is Ruth—Ruth Evans."

"My whole name is Gertrude Marion Morton," said Honey Bunch. "But every one calls me Honey Bunch. And I'm going to see

my cousin, too. She lives on a farm and her
name is Stub. Where does your cousin Laura
live?"

"She lives in Bayplace," answered Ruth.
"That's the seashore. What a funny name—
Stub! Is that her real name?"

"No—o. But she falls down when she stubs
her toe, and that's why they call her that," explained Honey Bunch. "What is Stub's real
name, Mother?"

"Oh, Honey Bunch, you know, if you'll
only stop to remember," laughed Mrs. Morton. "Her name is Mary Morton, dear."

"And I have a cousin who lives at the seashore, too," said Honey Bunch proudly.
"Julie. She came to my birthday party."

They had reached the mail box by this
time and Ruth lifted the lid and pulled out
several letters and a newspaper and two maga-
zines. Then she folded down the little
flag.

"Why do you bend it down?" asked Honey
Bunch, who thought this way of getting letters was much more exciting than to have the

postman bring them to the house and ring the doorbell.

"If you leave the flag up, the mail man will think there are letters in the box to be mailed," answered Ruth. "He doesn't like to go feeling around in the bottom of the box when there isn't anything there."

"Oh!" said Honey Bunch.

Mrs. Morton asked Ruth to walk with them down to the car, but Ruth said she had promised her mother to come straight back to the house.

"She wants to telephone to my brother, who lives in town, to go to meet my cousin, as soon as she knows what train she is coming on," explained Ruth. "So I'll scoot."

And up the lane she "scooted," her brown gingham skirts flapping as she ran. She could run fast, and in a few minutes she was out of sight.

"Dear me," said Mr. Morton, wiping his hands on a towel as Honey Bunch and her mother came around the front of the car, "I thought I saw two little girls. Didn't I? Did the fairies come and carry the other girl away?"

"That was Ruth Evans, Daddy," answered Honey Bunch. "She came down to get the letters out of the mail box. The mail man leaves them there once a day. Ruth has a cousin Laura who lives at the seashore, just like Julie. And the cousin is coming to see her when her mother telephones her brother to go to meet the train that the letter tells about."

Mr. Morton swung Honey Bunch into the seat and gave her a kiss.

"You must know all about Ruth Evans," he said teasingly. "So I really did see another little girl. I thought, perhaps, I was getting to be such an old daddy I needed glasses."

"You're not an old daddy!" exclaimed Honey Bunch.

"No, indeed," declared Mrs. Morton. "Here's a four-leaf clover I picked for you in the lane while Honey Bunch was talking to Ruth."

Mr. Morton put the clover in his watch

case and said it would bring him good luck.
Then, as the engine was "running beautifully"
he said, they started off again. But though
the car went as fast as it had before, Mr. Morton kept slowing up and once he stopped and
stood up to look back.

"What is the matter, David?" asked Honey
Bunch's mother. "Is anything coming up behind us?"

"No. But I begin to think I've taken the
wrong road," replied Mr. Morton. "Let's
have a look at the road maps. I should have
studied them before."

He spread the maps out on his lap, and
though Honey Bunch could not understand
the yellow and blue spots, Daddy and Mother
seemed to know what they meant. Mother
took a hairpin and followed a wide black line
clear across the paper.

"There's where I made the wrong turn,"
said Daddy, in a moment. "I'll turn the car
around—because the next cross road is at
least four miles ahead—and we'll go back. It
won't delay us more than half an hour."

CHAPTER V

NEW FRIENDS

Mr. Morton turned the car around and they went back as far as a painted white post Honey Bunch did not remember having seen before.

"That's the trouble," said her daddy when she pointed to the post. "We should have seen that—at least I should. Then I would have taken the right road. However, here we go." And he turned the car down another road which would, he explained, take them to Stub's house.

"What pretty clouds!" said Honey Bunch, when she looked across a field and saw big white clouds piled on top of each other. "Look, Mother, they're like the castles in my fairy-tale book."

"Yes, I see them," said Mrs. Morton, a lit-

tle anxiously. "I'm afraid they mean we are
going to have a thunder shower."

"It may go around us," said Mr. Morton,
glancing at the sky. "If we do get caught,
I'll drive in somewhere."

Honey Bunch thought the clouds were
lovely. They looked as though she could
plunge her hands up and down in them, as she
sometimes did in Mrs. Miller's soapsuds.
That is, if she could get near enough to the sky
to reach the clouds. Honey Bunch was sure
that if Daddy drove straight across the fields
to the spot where the sky touched the earth,
she could grab a piece of the clouds. But
then, Daddy was in a hurry to get to the farm,
she knew, and it wouldn't be fair to ask him to
drive so far out of his way.

"Now they're dark," said Honey Bunch
suddenly, staring at the beautiful white clouds
which had turned black while she watched
them.

"See how fast they go," said Mrs. Morton,
who was watching the clouds, too. "Almost
as fast as the car goes."

"What makes the clouds move?" asked
Honey Bunch.

"The wind, dear," replied her mother.
"Hark! I hear thunder."

Honey Bunch listened. Far away she
heard a rumble and a muttering.

"It's back of the clouds, Mother," she said.

"We'll not get wet," Mr. Morton said, not
even looking at the clouds again. "I'm not
going to stop to put on the side curtains. I
think there is a farmhouse just ahead and
we'll run into the barn and wait till the shower
is over."

The white clouds were every one black now
and the wind was blowing hard. Honey
Bunch could see the trees rocking back and
forth. The thunder sounded nearer and little
jagged streaks of light darted across the sky
in front of the automobile.

"How glad all the little green growing
things will be to get the rain," said Mrs. Morton. "I'm sure they are thirsty for a drink of
water."

"And we'll not have any more dust to-day,"

declared Mr. Morton. "All the rest of the
way to the farm we'll have a dustless road.
Aha, there's the farmhouse chimney."

Honey Bunch stood up to look. There *was*
a chimney showing through a clump of trees.

Pat! Pat! Pat! went something softly.

"What's that?" asked Honey Bunch.
"What's that funny noise?"

"It is the rain," answered her mother.
"You hear the drops striking the leaves. Do
hurry, Daddy, so we won't get wet."

The car leaped ahead and in another minute they were opposite a barn. There was a
man standing in the doorway and as soon as
he saw them he pushed the sliding door back
and Mr. Morton ran the car through the doorway into the nice dry barn.

"Hello!" said the man pleasantly. "Most
caught you, didn't it?"

He was a little old man and he seemed glad
to see them. He opened the door for Honey
Bunch and her mother to step down and the
first thing he said to Honey Bunch was:

"Do you like kittens?"

"Oh, yes!" replied Honey Bunch, looking at the old man as though she thought he might have a kitten in the pockets of his overalls.

"Well, Mother has some, up at the house," said the little old man. "If you all will come on up, she'll be right glad to see you."

"Perhaps we had better wait here," said Mr. Morton. "Is it far to the house?"

"Just a step," replied the old man. "You can run between the drops."

Honey Bunch laughed. She didn't see how Daddy could run between the little fine drops of rain. The old man laughed, too.

"Mother loves to have company," he said. "She's seen your car come in. I know she has the kettle on by this time and is getting out the cookies. She'll never forgive me if I don't bring you up to the house."

"All right, let's run for it," said Mr. Morton, picking up Honey Bunch. "Come, Edith—it isn't raining hard yet."

The house was not far away and they all ran, Daddy carrying Honey Bunch. As they reached the front porch the door was opened

and a tiny little old lady bounced out, waving
her apron and smiling.

"Come right in and set a spell," she cried.
"Are you wet? Are you cold? I'll have a
cup of hot tea for you in a minute. Come out
in the kitchen where the fire is."

Talking every minute, the old lady led them
into the largest kitchen Honey Bunch had
ever seen. Although it was summer, the room
was not too warm, for the shower had brought
a cold wind with it, and when people are wet
a fire feels very comfortable indeed. There
was a fire in the big stove and a teakettle send-
ing out white clouds of steam and in the middle of the kitchen a round table spread with a
white cloth.

"I know you're hungry," said the old lady
cheerfully. "Folks are always hungry when
they're driving. I'm so sorry I didn't know
you were coming, or I could have cooked
something special."

In two minutes they felt as though they
had always known the little old lady and
the little old man. Their names, they said,

were Popover—Mr. and Mrs. Popover.

"Just remember popovers and you'll remember us," said the old lady, who could certainly talk faster than any one Honey Bunch had ever known.

Indeed, everything Mrs. Popover did, was done quickly. She talked fast and she walked fast and she had cups of tea poured out for her visitors—with a glass of milk for Honey Bunch—and had brought out a basket of striped yellow and white kittens and three pictures of her grandchildren and then sat down and knitted, almost before Mrs. Morton had taken off Honey Bunch's hat and unloosened her own linen coat.

"Such darling kitties!" cried Honey Bunch, sitting down on the floor beside the basket. "Have they any names?"

"To be sure," said Mrs. Popover, knitting away as fast as she talked. "One is named Topaz—that's the one you are stroking now. Then there is Emerald and Ruby and Pearl. Peter, pass the child a cookie."

Mr. Popover brought the plate of cookies

to Honey Bunch who took one and went on petting the kittens.

"I'm going to give Topaz to my grandson, Cornelius, just as soon as the kittens are old enough to give away," said Mrs. Popover. "Pearl is for my granddaughter, Lucy, and Emerald is for the baby, Albert."

"But there is Ruby," Honey Bunch reminded her. "Haven't you any more grandchildren, Mrs. Popover?"

"Oh, Father and I will keep Ruby," answered the old lady. "The mother cat, Jewel, would feel lonely if we didn't keep one kitten."

Honey Bunch asked where the mother cat was.

"Out in the barn most likely," said Mr. Popover, who was eating cookies as though he liked them very much. "Jewel is a great mouser and she patrols the barn as regularly as a policeman."

"I'm right glad you dropped in," declared Mrs. Popover, beaming at her guests and clicking her needles faster than ever. Father

and I get lonely with no one to talk to. I
often tell him we ought to borrow some children to stay with us. Our daughter and her
children live fifty miles away and we don't
see them as often as we'd like."

While the Popovers talked, the thunder
storm was "storming," as Honey Bunch said.
The wind rattled the shutters of the farmhouse and the rain poured down. The thunder sounded directly over their heads, but no
one seemed to pay much attention to the storm.
Mr. Popover and Mr. Morton were talking
about farming and Mrs. Popover was showing Mrs. Morton her patchwork quilts—she
took her upstairs to show her those—and
Honey Bunch played with the kittens and
loved them. They were too busy to listen to
the wind and the rain.

"It is getting lighter now," said Mr. Morton, walking over to the window. "I think
we can be going on in a few moments. Honey
Bunch, can you find Mother, and tell her I
am going out to the barn to start the car?"

"You go right out into that hall and up the

stairs," said Mr. Popover to Honey Bunch. "You'll find the ladies talking about basting threads and thimbles in the front room, I'll bet a cookie."

Honey Bunch laughed and trotted into the wide, square, front hall. She went up the stairs that twisted and as soon as she reached the upstairs hall she heard Mrs. Popover talking.

"Come right in, dear," said the old lady. "I've been showing your mother my quilts. I don't suppose you ever made patchwork, did you? When I was a little girl that was the first needlework we did."

Honey Bunch looked at the gay quilts spread across the bed. There were stars and wheels and diamonds, all beautifully stitched together. There was every color of the rainbow in those quilts, too.

"How pretty!" said Honey Bunch. "Did you make them, Mrs. Popover?"

"Every one," said the old lady proudly. "I've won twenty prizes at the State fair for my quilt patterns."

When Honey Bunch said that Daddy had gone out to the barn and that he wanted them to be ready to start in a few moments, Mrs. Popover seemed much disappointed.

"I hoped it would settle down into a steady rain, so you could stay all night," she said. "I'd have fried chicken for supper if I thought you'd stay."

"Oh, they will be expecting us at the farm," replied Honey Bunch's mother. "We couldn't stay over a night—though it is lovely of you to be so hospitable."

"Well, I like plenty of people around," answered Mrs. Popover, folding up the quilts. "When Father and I were younger we had summer boarders a good deal. They were good company, but they used to rile me because they couldn't remember our names. We were always getting letters addressed to Mr. Muffin or Mrs. Biscuit, and it got on my nerves, though I s'pose that was silly."

Honey Bunch and her mother laughed at the idea of a letter addressed to "Mrs. Biscuit," and Mrs. Popover, too, laughed good-

naturedly. She followed them out to the barn
and begged them to stop in if they ever drove
past again.

"Stop on your way home, at least," she
urged. "Stop off here for dinner when you
go back."

Mr. Morton said they would and that
promise seemed to cheer Mr. and Mrs. Popover so much they smiled and waved their
hands quite gaily as the car went down the
road.

"They're just lonely," said Honey Bunch's
mother. "They ought to have some one who
is young and gay and happy come and live
with them."

"Some one like Honey Bunch," said Honey
Bunch's daddy, smiling at his little girl. "But
we can't spare her."

The rain had stopped entirely now and the
fields were fresh and green as though just
washed. And that was what the rain had
done—washed them. There was no dust in
the road, either, and theirs seemed to be the
only car out. Honey Bunch was thinking

about Mr. and Mrs. Popover and the kittens when her daddy slowed down and turned into a cemented drive that was bordered on each side by beautiful blue iris.

"All out for Broad Acres!" called Mr. Morton briskly.

CHAPTER VI

BROAD ACRES

"OH, Honey Bunch! I thought you never were coming!" shouted Stub, flying down the lawn.

She dashed up to the car and tumbled in, hugging Mrs. Morton and Honey Bunch and trying to tell them how glad she was to see them.

"Here, here," said Mr. Morton, leaning over the back of the seat to kiss her. "Where's Mother, Stub? And do we drive on in or get out here?"

"Drive on around," said Stub, climbing over beside Mr. Morton. "Mother is on the porch and Daddy and Michael are out in the barn."

Mr. Morton followed the cement drive around to the side porch where Stub's mother came down the steps to meet them.

"There's a telegram for you, David," said Stub's mother, lifting Honey Bunch down and kissing Mrs. Morton. "It came this morning."

Stub's mother was "Aunt Carol" to Honey Bunch, and she was as gentle and calm as Stub was hurried and excited. Honey Bunch thought Aunt Carol was very pretty, with her soft, dark hair and blue eyes and she liked to hear her low, even voice.

"I'll run the car out to the barn and come back," said Honey Bunch's daddy. "I've an idea what that telegram says. I thought I could get in a week's vacation, but it seems not."

"Come on, we'll go, too," said Stub, pulling Honey Bunch back into the car. "You haven't seen the barn yet."

Mr. Morton laughed and said that Honey Bunch had not seen anything yet.

"But she will know every corner of the farm, with you to show her, Stub," he said. "Hello, here's Rand."

Stub's daddy stood in the doorway of the barn and beckoned them to drive in.

"Park right here on the barn floor," he said. "Give the horses something to look at when they're not working."

Uncle Rand had a jolly face and eyes that twinkled. Honey Bunch decided that he looked as though he could make up poetry, and she thought she would tell him about Mrs. Miller's burned fingers as soon as she had a chance.

"Well, Honey Bunch, welcome to the farm," said Uncle Rand, lifting her out of the car. "Carol tell you about the telegram, David?" he asked, shaking hands with Honey Bunch's daddy.

"Yes, thanks," said Mr. Morton. "It means I'll have to go back to-morrow, I'm afraid. Oh, here is Buffy. Honey Bunch, come and shake hands with Buffy."

A large Shepherd dog bounced up to them and held out his paw to Honey Bunch very politely. She shook hands with him and patted his head. When Buffy sat down he was as tall as Honey Bunch. That is, his head was on a level with hers.

"Stub," said Uncle Rand, "we're going up to the house. Supper will be ready in half an hour. You and Honey Bunch come in when Michael does and you won't be late."

"Yes, Daddy," answered Stub.

The two daddies went away and Stub took Honey Bunch by the hand.

"I'll show you all the nicest places in the barn," she said. "But first come and talk to Michael."

She led Honey Bunch through the barn till they came to another door. This was twice as wide as the one they had driven through and Honey Bunch was surprised to find, when she looked through it, that she was upstairs.

"We didn't come up any stairs," she said to Stub. "But this is the second floor, isn't it?"

"There's a basement under the barn," explained Stub. "You don't see it from the front of the barn. Michael! Michael! here's my cousin!" she called.

Honey Bunch looked down and into a thin

brown face with the merriest smile flashing
up at her she had ever seen. She smiled back
at once—every one smiled at Michael.

"Hello, Miss Honey Bunch!" said Michael,
waving a cornstalk at her. "I've heard all
kinds of nice things about you."

"What are you doing, Michael?" asked
Stub. "Can we jump down?"

"Certainly not," said Michael promptly.
"It's soaking wet down here. I'm spreading
out dry stalks because your father wants the
cows to have a dry place to-night. That was
a mighty heavy shower we had."

"We saw it," said Honey Bunch.

Then she jumped a little, for a cold nose
touched her hand. It was Buffy, who wanted
to look through the door, too.

"Come on, we'll go up in the haymow," said
Stub, who never could stand still a moment.
"I'll show you how I can walk across a beam."

She pulled Honey Bunch up the little shaky
ladder that led to the haymow and Buffy sat
down on the floor to wait for them. He was
too fat to climb ladders, and he knew it.

"Now you sit down and watch me," said Stub.

She was a year older than Honey Bunch and as strong and sturdy as little girls are who live in the country all the year around and play outdoors in every kind of weather. Her daddy often said that Stub was "built like a little football," by which he meant that she was not easily hurt and that bumps and knocks did not seem to bother her or discourage her.

"You watch," said Stub, scrambling up on a heavy beam that ran across the haymow.

Honey Bunch sat down on the slippery hay and watched. She thought that Stub was very brave to walk across the beam so high in the air and she was quite sure that she, Honey Bunch, would never do such a thing. She didn't even want to try.

"It's just as easy!" called Stub. "Some day I mean to walk on the beam that is under the cupola—when Michael isn't around to stop me."

Alas for Stub's pride. She had almost reached the end of the beam and was thinking

about turning around to walk back when she
stubbed her toe—poor Stub, she *would* stub
her toe, no matter how careful she was—and,
losing her balance, down she crashed, fortu-
nately into the hay.

"Are you hurt?" cried Honey Bunch,
scrambling over to her. "Stub, did you hurt
yourself?"

"No, I'm not hurt," answered Stub, rather
breathlessly. "I did come down kind of hard,
though, didn't I? Maybe it's time for us to
go in to supper."

"Stub!" called some one just at that moment. "Stub! Stubby!"

"That's Liny," said Stub, standing up and
brushing off her dress. "She's calling us to
supper. Come on, Honey Bunch."

Down the ladder tumbled Stub and Honey
Bunch followed her more carefully. She was
wondering who "Liny" was, and as they
walked over the grass to the house, Stub told
her.

"Liny is the hired girl," she said. "She
makes the best turnovers you ever ate."

That reminded Honey Bunch of the old
man and old lady, Mr. and Mrs. Popover, and
she told Stub about them. By this time they
had reached the house. They went in, to find
the grown-ups already seated at the table.
Liny, who was a short, fat girl, whisked them
into her kitchen and had their faces and hands
washed and their hair brushed almost before
Honey Bunch knew what she was doing.
There was a little room next to the kitchen
which had been made over into a bathroom, to
save busy folk the trouble of going upstairs to
the large bathroom.

"Now run along," said Liny kindly, giving
them a little push when she had finished.
"I'm going to prayer meeting to-night and
I don't want to be late with the supper
dishes."

Honey Bunch was so tired from the long
drive and the excitement of the day that she
hardly knew when Mother took her upstairs
to put her into the big, four-posted bed in the
square room with five windows which was to
be her bedroom. She did not know, either,

how long she had been asleep when Daddy
woke her up by kissing her.

"Is it morning?" asked Honey Bunch sleepily. "Do I get up right away?"

"No, dear, not time to get up for you," replied her daddy, hugging her tightly. "Good-
by, darling. Daddy will come back as soon
as he can."

"Good-by," murmured sleepy little Honey
Bunch without knowing what she said.

She turned over on the nice cool pillow and
went fast asleep again.

By and by she woke up and found Mother
had been up and dressed for several hours and
Daddy had gone away.

"The telegram called him to New York,
dear," Mother explained, sitting down on the
bed by Honey Bunch. "He will go back to
Barham in the car and then on to New York
by train. And he thinks he'll come and get
us before our six weeks are up."

Honey Bunch missed her daddy and she
was sorry he had to go back to the dusty city.
But there was so much to see and do on the

farm that she couldn't be sorry very long.
There was sure to be something interesting going on wherever Stub was, and Honey Bunch
thought her cousin was a very wonderful little girl.

"She isn't afraid of anything," said Honey
Bunch to Michael one morning. "I don't like
the white cow, but Stub will pat her right on
the nose."

"Well, Stub has always lived on a farm and
she is used to cows," said Michael kindly. "I
dare say there are plenty of things in the city
that would surprise her."

Honey Bunch did not really think that Stub
would be surprised at anything. A girl who
couldn't be surprised by a cow, thought
Honey Bunch, wouldn't be surprised at—at—
well, not even subway trains.

"Come on," said Stub, rushing out of the
kitchen door. "Hurry up, Honey Bunch.
We want to go down to the brook before dinner time. The tax assessor is coming to dinner and Mother says I must keep this dress
clean, so we can't go wading."

"It's too cold, anyway, to go wading yet," said Michael, who was painting a flower box for Stub's mother.

"What's a tax assessor?" asked Honey Bunch, as the two little girls hurried down to the brook.

"He's a man," explained Stub. "Daddy knows him. His name is Mr. Kelly. He always comes to our house for dinner when he is in Elmville. Want to race me to the brook, Honey Bunch?"

Honey Bunch was willing, and away they went, pellmell, down the hill, over the road, and into the tall grass.

"Look out for stones!" panted Stub, and just as she said that she tripped and went tumbling headlong.

"Oh, my! Your dress!" cried Honey Bunch, more worried about Stub's clean frock than her cousin's arms or legs. Indeed Stub seldom hurt herself, but she surely did spoil a great many dresses.

"It's all right," said Stub hastily, sitting up

and rubbing her elbows. "I've just pulled some of the gathers out."

Honey Bunch looked at the dress doubtfully. It touched the ground when Stub stood up because she had pulled the skirt loose from the waist. There was a great streak of dirt across the front, too, and Honey Bunch was sure Aunt Carol would not call it a clean dress now.

"I don't see why I can't fall backward," complained the unlucky Stub. "I always tear my dresses in front where they show. But I guess we can mend this before Mother sees it. Come on, Honey Bunch, let's go up to my room and we'll sew it up. The dirt will brush off with a wet rag. I know it will."

They climbed the hill again and went in at the side door and up the back stairs to Stub's room without meeting any one.

CHAPTER VII

LINY'S PICTURE

STUB had a little workbasket of her own, with needles and thread and a shining pair of blunt-pointed scissors in it. She did not like to sew, but her mother said that perhaps if she had her own basket she might use it instead of pulling all the spools out of the large mending basket and tangling up the tape measure with the darning cotton.

"Can you mend it without taking it off?" asked Honey Bunch, watching Stub as she threaded a needle with black thread.

Stub's dress was pink, but she thought black thread was stronger than any other kind, so she used that.

"I can't sew it, but you can," said Stub. "Here, take this and don't stick it in me."

Poor Honey Bunch stuck out her tongue as she always did when she was trying to do her best, and took the large needle Stub handed her. She didn't know how the dress ought to be mended, but Stub did.

"You run the needle along and kind of pick up all the gathers," she directed. "Then you sew it fast to the waist."

Honey Bunch ran the needle in and out, in and out, and when she had all the gingham bunched up she took one long stitch to fasten it to the waist.

"Ow! Ouch!" screamed Stub, dancing up and down. "Ouch! Oh, you ran that right into me!"

"I—I didn't mean to," said Honey Bunch. "Did it hurt you very much, Stub?"

"Yes, it did," answered Stub. "But go on. I'll hold my breath in and maybe you won't do it again."

Though Honey Bunch hurried as fast as she could, Stub was quite purple in the face from holding her breath before she had finished.

"I don't think it looks very good," said Stub, snipping the thread with her scissors. "But it will do, I guess. Now I'll wash the

dirt off with a wet cloth and then we'll go
down. Liny must have dinner 'most ready."

Stub took one of the towels in the bathroom
and soaked one end of it in warm water.
Then she scrubbed her dress with it. The
more she scrubbed, the darker the streak of
dirt grew.

"You'll get the whole dress wet," said
Honey Bunch. "I don't believe you can get
it off, Stub."

"I don't believe I can, either," sighed Stub.
"Maybe Liny will lend me an apron. A nice,
clean apron will be all right, even if the tax
assessor is coming."

The two little girls ran downstairs and
peeped out on the front porch. There sat a
stout, red-faced man, talking to Stub's father.

"That's Mr. Kelly," said Stub. "Come on.
Liny's in the kitchen."

Liny was in the kitchen. She was putting
pretty green lettuce leaves on a plate and talking to Michael, who sat on the back steps with
Buffy.

"My land!" said Liny, when she saw Stub

HONEY BUNCH AND STUB ENJOY THE SWING.

Honey Bunch: Her First Days on the Farm.   Page 79

and Honey Bunch. "Dinner will be on the table in five minutes, and look at you!"

"Will you lend me an apron, Liny?" said Stub, coaxingly. "This dress isn't very clean."

"Michael," said Liny, "I ask you to look at these children."

"What's the matter with them?" asked Michael, standing up to look in through the screen door.

"Matter?" repeated Liny. "Why, Stub's dress is a sight! It's wet and dirty and sewed up with black thread in stitches you could see a mile away. And her face is black and Honey Bunch has a streak of dirt across her nose and I never saw such hands in my life! And company to dinner, too!"

Honey Bunch was surprised to hear she had a dirty face. She had been so busy helping Stub that she had forgotten to wash her own face and hands.

"Michael, you chop me some ice," said Liny, drying her hands on a clean towel. "I won't be a minute."

And in hardly more than a minute, Liny had Honey Bunch soaking her hands in the little bathroom off the kitchen while she hustled Stub into a clean blue dress that had been ironed that very morning and was lying on top of the clothes basket ready to be carried upstairs. Then Liny brushed Stub's hair and washed her face and tied Honey Bunch's ribbon again and dusted off their sandals and gave them each a clean pocket handerchief from the basket of clean clothes.

"Now then go out and sit down in a rocking chair and don't let me hear a word from you till dinner is on the table," said Liny, hurrying back to her kitchen.

So Honey Bunch and Stub went out and spoke to Mr. Kelly, and no one would ever have thought that two such clean, cool, neat little girls could ever have been the least bit untidy.

It was a very good dinner—at Broad Acres they had dinner in the middle of the day instead of at night, as most people did in Barham—but neither Honey Bunch nor Stub could talk very much. Mr. Kelly talked a great deal and Stub's daddy talked to him and her mother did, too, and Honey Bunch's Mother. Honey Bunch and Stub talked to each other a little, and they were glad when they were excused after the dessert had been served.

They went out to the swing and stayed there till they saw Mr. Kelly ride away in his little red automobile. Then they went around to see if Liny would play croquet with them. Stub had been delighted with the croquet set. Michael had set it out, and sometimes he and Liny would play when they were not too busy.

Both Honey Bunch and Stub liked Michael and Liny very much. They were always cheerful and they seemed to have a good time, though they did a great deal of work. Sunday afternoons Michael took Liny driving in a runabout. Stub told Honey Bunch that was the name of the shiny wagon harnessed to the shiny black horse.

"Michael is saving money to buy an auto-

mobile," said Stub. "But Daddy won't have
a car; he likes to drive horses."

This afternoon when Honey Bunch and
Stub went around to ask Liny to come out and
play croquet, they found her reading a letter.
She was putting away the silver with one hand
and holding the letter in the other and she
laughed when she saw Honey Bunch's blue
eyes staring at her.

"I ought not to try to do two things at
once," said Liny, "and I'll put the rest of the
dishes in place before I read this letter again.
Would you like to see a picture of my brothers, Honey Bunch?"

"Oh, yes!" said Honey Bunch, and Stub,
who had heard of Liny's brothers, came close
to see the photographs, too.

Honey Bunch looked at the picture Liny
gave her. She saw two young men standing
very straight and very tall. They looked seri-
ous. The taller one had his hand on the
shoulder of the other and they were staring
out of the picture straight into the eyes of
whoever should be looking at them.

"The tall one is Walter," said Liny proudly. "And the shorter one—though he is almost six feet high—is George."

"Will they come to dinner?" asked Honey Bunch, who thought that if a tax assessor came, any one was likely to come to one of Liny's good dinners.

"Oh, ho!" laughed Stub. "They couldn't come, could they, Liny? They live in South America!"

"But Liny lives here," said Honey Bunch. "Uncle Peter is Mother's brother—Mother told me so—and he doesn't live in South America. Brothers and sisters live near each other. Don't they, Liny?"

"Not always, dearie," said Liny. "Walter and George went to South America over two years ago. I don't expect them home before another two years are up. They are trying to make money and save it. Then, perhaps, we'll have a home together some day."

Liny stared at the picture a moment, then put it down on the table. She folded up the letter and placed that in her apron pocket and began to carry the clean dishes into the dining room and to put them away in the china cupboard.

"Liny, will you play one game of croquet?" asked Stub. "Just one before you go upstairs to rest your bones?"

Liny had a few hours to herself every afternoon, and she had once told Stub that she "rested her bones" in that interval.

"All right, I will if you'll get Michael to hammer on the head of that orange mallet," said Liny. "I can't abide a mallet that comes off when you're playing with it. Tell him to hammer it hard."

Stub ran away to get Michael to mend the orange mallet—orange was Liny's favorite color and she always chose it when she played croquet—and Honey Bunch wandered into the living room to look at the sun and moon clock while she waited for the game.

The sun and moon clock fascinated Honey Bunch. It was a very, very old clock and Uncle Rand said it had belonged to her great great grandmother. It was short and fat and

dark and it had a sun and moon and little
stars sprinkled over the square patch of glass
above the clock face and sometimes it told
when the moon changed. It didn't always,
for it was such an old clock it didn't always
work. Uncle Rand said that clocks grew tired
of working just as people did, and when they
were old they liked plenty of rest.

"Liny!" Honey Bunch heard Stub come
running into the kitchen. "Liny, Michael has
found the white hen's nest! It's up in the
haymow and he says there are seven eggs
there."

"I'm coming!" answered Liny, and Honey
Bunch heard the screen door slam as she ran
after Stub.

Honey Bunch ran out into the kitchen, in-
tending to follow Liny and see the white hen's
nest, too; but as soon as she went into the
kitchen she saw the photograph of Liny's
brothers lying on the floor. Liny had brushed
it off with her apron as she ran out of the door.

"Where'll I put it?" said Honey Bunch to
herself, picking it up. "Liny won't want to

lose it. I know! I'll put it on top of the sun and moon clock."

Into the living room she trotted and dragged a chair over to the mantel. She had to stand on her tiptoes to reach the clock, but she did manage to put the picture on the top. Then she climbed down and raced out to the barn where she found Michael and Liny and Stub and one indignant white hen very much put out because her nest had been found and her seven round eggs she had thought to keep a secret.

By the time Michael had shut up the hen in the hen-house and Liny had put away the eggs in her egg basket and one game of croquet to satisfy Stub had been played, it was time for Liny to think about putting on a clean dress and getting supper.

"I'll go down and pick up enough green apples for apple sauce first," she decided. "Do you two want to come along?"

Stub and Honey Bunch did want to go, and they helped Liny gather the apples and then followed her back to the house. Just as Liny

was going upstairs, she remembered her
photograph.

"What did I do with Walter and George's
picture?" she said. "Don't tell me I left it in
my apron pocket, for if I did, it's dropped
out."

"It was on the floor," cried Honey Bunch
eagerly. "I found it and I put it on top of the
sun and moon clock for you."

Liny hurried into the living room.

"Your mother must have taken it off," she
said, glancing at the mantel. "It isn't there."

But neither Honey Bunch's mother nor
Stub's mother had seen the picture. When
Liny asked them, they said they had not
touched it. They did not know Liny had re-
ceived a photograph from South America.

CHAPTER VIII

IN THE ORCHARD

"But, Mother," said Honey Bunch earnestly, "I put it right on top of the sun and moon clock."

"Then it must have dropped down behind it," said Mrs. Morton, and she and Aunt Carol moved the clock and everything on the mantel shelf, but there was no picture anywhere to be found.

"I'm just as sorry as I can be, Liny," said Aunt Carol. "Can't you get another one?"

"It's the only one they had taken," sighed poor Liny. "Well, it's my own fault for not taking better care of it. Don't you cry, Honey Bunch; you couldn't help it. Maybe it will turn up again, anyway."

But although Liny cleaned the living room the next day and swept and shook and beat every rug and curtain and pillow and dusted

every vase and bit of woodwork and every
ornament on the shelf, she did not find the picture. It seemed to have disappeared "like
magic," Liny said.

"I stood on a chair and I put it on the
clock," said Honey Bunch over and over. "I
found the picture on the floor and I meant to
save it. I don't see where it went."

For as long as a week, Honey Bunch and
Liny and Stub hunted for the picture and then
they gave it up and said it must be lost. There
were so many interesting things to do on the
farm that even Honey Bunch couldn't be expected to stay in the house and hunt for a miss-
ing photograph, though she was a persevering
little girl and did not like to give up.

"Where are you going, Michael?" asked
Honey Bunch, one sunny morning.

She was sitting on the front porch waiting
for Stub, and Michael had come whistling
around the corner of the house. He carried a
roll of wire over his shoulder and had some
tools in his hand.

"Going to mend the orchard fence," answered he, smiling. "The apples are beginning to get ripe and your uncle thinks some of the neighbors' young pigs have been in rooting for them."

"But why don't the pigs stay at home?" asked Honey Bunch. "They mustn't come over here and eat Uncle Rand's apples."

"Well, somebody doesn't mend his fences," explained Michael. "But that isn't my fault. I aim to make ours tight, and then we won't have to worry."

"We're coming, Michael," said Stub, bouncing out of the door and almost falling over Honey Bunch. "Where are you going?"

That was just like Stub. She always made up her mind to go before she found out where she was going.

"All right, come along if you want to," said Michael. "I like company."

Honey Bunch loved to go to the orchard. She liked the grass and the smell of honeysuckle which grew along the fence. She liked the trees which were so low and easy to climb that a little girl could scramble up into them without a bit of trouble. Oh, the orchard was the nicest place to play, no doubt of that!

This morning they found apples lying on the ground. There had been a shower in the night and the wind had knocked a good many off.

"Now look here," said Michael, putting down his wire. "You are not to eat a dozen apples and make yourselves sick. They're hardly ripe enough to be good, you know."

"But here's a ripe sweet apple, Michael," urged Stub. "Look, it's just as soft! And here's another for Honey Bunch!"

"You'll probably find a bad spot in it somewhere," said Michael. "Eat one, then, just one! Will you promise, Stub? And look out for Honey Bunch?"

"Yes, of course," replied Stub, biting into her apple with her sharp little white teeth. "I guess I know about green apples, Michael."

"Perhaps you do," said Michael. "I remember the last time you were sick. Now I'm going to work. Why don't you pick up

the green apples and put them in a pile for
Liny? She'll give us hot apple sauce and bis-
cuits for supper then, perhaps."

Honey Bunch and Stub thought this was a
very good plan. They began to hunt under
the trees for fallen apples, and each one they
found they carried back to a tree near
the piece of fence that Michael was mending.

"What do green apples do to you, Stub?"
asked Honey Bunch.

"They double you up," answered Stub.

"Did you ever eat any?" asked Honey
Bunch, looking at a green apple she had found
as though it might bite her and double her up
on the spot.

"Twice," answered Stub. "Once when I
was little and didn't know green apples would
make you sick, and last year when I thought
the apples were ripe and they weren't."

"Yes, and who told you they were not ripe
and you wouldn't take his word for it?" said
Michael, who had overheard her.

"You did," admitted Stub. "But I'm much

older now and I know a lot more. Green apples make you *so* sick, Honey Bunch."

Honey Bunch finished her nice sweet apple and said she wouldn't eat a green apple, not for anything!

"There! we've picked all the apples there are," said Stub suddenly. "Let's climb a tree and play ship."

Stub loved to play ship. She had taught Honey Bunch the game, too. They each climbed into a tree and sat as far out on a limb as they could climb and then they bounced softly up and down. That, Stub said, was the ship rocking at sea.

"I wonder if Julie goes sailing in real boats," said Honey Bunch, as she made her apple tree ship rock up and down.

Julie, you know was her cousin—and also Stub's cousin—who lived at the seashore.

"Of course she does," replied Stub, though she really didn't know whether Julie went sailing or not. "I wish I lived at the seashore."

Bang! Bang! went Michael's hammer, as

he pounded nails into the post to hold the wire.

"Michael!" called Stub. "Oh, Michael, wouldn't you like to live at the seashore?"

"Certainly not," replied Michael, taking the nails out of his mouth so that he could speak more plainly. "I like to live in the country. That's why I do. Stub, where's Buffy?"

"Why—why, he's shut up in the wagon house," said Stub. "I forgot to let him out. Are you going to, Michael?"

"I'm going up after more nails, but if you want Buffy out, you'll have to go and do it," said Michael. "That's the second time you've forgotten him. I am not going to the wagon house, only to the tool box."

"You wait for me, Honey Bunch," said Stub, climbing down from her tree and starting to run.

Stub knew that Michael was not to be coaxed or teased. She always shut Buffy in the wagon house to keep him from barking at the mail carrier, and she was supposed to let

the dog out the moment the mail had passed.
Alas, Stub sometimes forgot him and he
would be shut up in the stuffy wagon house
till some one went there and found him.
Michael knew that the best way to help Stub
remember her pet was to let her go and open
the door for him. If Michael did it for her,
Stub might never learn to be thoughtful.

So Michael went to get more nails and Stub
ran to let out Buffy and Honey Bunch was
left alone in the sunny orchard.

As she swung up and down on her branch,
she saw something moving near the fence
where Michael had been working.

"Are you a little pig?" called Honey Bunch
softly, leaning down and trying to see under
the honeysuckle vine.

Two red, dirty and indignant small faces
peered out at her.

"Don't you dare call us names!" said a voice
that sounded very much like a small boy's
voice. "Aren't you ashamed of yourself!"

"I didn't know you were there," said Honey
Bunch. "Excuse me. Michael said little pigs

came through the fence and that's why I thought you were one. The pigs ate our apples before the fence was mended."

"We were hunting for the hole," said the boy who had spoken. "Do you live here?"

"I'm Honey Bunch," answered the little girl. "I'm visiting Stub. She's my cousin. This is Uncle Rand's farm, you know."

"I'm Guy and he's Ted," the boy replied, beginning to climb over the fence. "We're boarding at Mr. Phillips'. But he won't let us in his orchard."

"Gee, the apples are ripe, aren't they?" said the other boy, Ted, running over to the tree where Honey Bunch and Stub had piled the apples for Liny to make into apple sauce.

"No, they're not!" cried Honey Bunch, slipping down from the tree. "They're green! Michael said so. If you eat them, they'll double you up."

"Nothing can double me up," boasted Guy. "Anyway, these apples are ripe. I can squeeze them."

"Michael said they'd make us sick," argued

Honey Bunch. "I guess he knows. Stub ate one sweet apple and so did I, but that's all that were under the sweet apple tree."

"Then, if these aren't ripe, what are you saving 'em for?" asked Ted, picking one of the apples up and starting to eat it.

Honey Bunch stared at him. She expected him to double up before her eyes.

"They're for apple sauce for supper," she said.

"Well, if apples in apple sauce don't make you sick, they won't raw," declared Guy. "Come on, Ted, fill your pockets."

"They're Uncle Rand's apples!" exclaimed Honey Bunch. "And they will, too, make you sick. See if they don't."

But the two boys stuffed their pockets with the apples and filled their caps and then climbed the fence and ran away before Michael and Stub and Buffy came back together to the orchard.

"There were two boys here and they took a lot of apples," said Honey Bunch. "I think it's just like stealing. And won't apples raw

make you sick when apple sauce won't,
Michael?"

"Sure," said Michael. "Might as well say
that if a raw potato isn't good for you, a baked
one isn't, either. Cooking makes all the dif-
ference in the world. I'm sorry those kids
got away with the green stuff, though it
wasn't stealing, Honey Bunch. Apples that
lie on the ground, in the country, are free
for the asking, and most times without—to
boys."

That night Aunt Carol was called to the
telephone from the supper table. When she
came back she smiled at Honey Bunch. She
had heard all about the morning in the
orchard.

"Mrs. Phillips just telephoned me," said
Aunt Carol, "that those two little boys who
are spending the summer with her have been
dreadfully sick all the afternoon. They had
to send for the doctor, because their mother
was so frightened about them. She says she
doesn't think they will take green apples from
our orchard again. Mr. Phillips tried to keep

them away from his orchard till the fruit
should be ripe enough to eat."

"Aunt Carol," asked Honey Bunch earnestly, "did they double up?"

"I didn't ask Mrs. Phillips, but I shouldn't
be surprised if they did," replied Aunt Carol,
while Uncle Rand leaned back in his chair
and laughed till the tears came into his eyes.

CHAPTER IX

BRAVE STUB

EVERY time Honey Bunch went into the living room she looked up at the sun and moon clock. She thought she might see the photograph of Walter and George, Liny's brothers, but she never did.

"I don't see how a picture could get lost," said Honey Bunch thoughtfully.

She was standing by the window, waiting for Stub. She often had to wait for Stub, who was constantly getting into accidents and needing clean frocks and dry shoes. This time Stub had caught her dress on a nail and her mother had sent her upstairs to put on another.

Uncle Rand sat at the flat-topped desk in the living room, writing. Honey Bunch wondered if he were busy.

"What are you thinking about, chicken?"

he asked her, putting down his pen and sealing an envelope with a splotch of red sealing wax.

"About Mrs. Miller," answered Honey Bunch. "She washes our clothes, you know. I told the poetry to her."

"What poetry?" Uncle Rand asked, hunting in his little brass box where he kept postage stamps.

"The poetry you made up for Stub to say when she stubs her toe," replied Honey Bunch. "Could you make up some for Mrs. Miller, Uncle Rand? I told her perhaps you could."

"Well, now, I don't know what kind of poetry Mrs. Miller likes or needs," said Uncle Rand slowly. "It is very important, you know, Honey Bunch, to know that."

"I know!" cried Honey Bunch eagerly. "I know just the kind. She needs some to say when she burns her thumb! She burns her thumb as much as Stub falls down! She said so, Uncle Rand."

"All right, Mrs. Miller shall have a verse," declared Uncle Rand. "Let me think a moment."

He leaned back in his chair and Honey Bunch sat as still as a little mouse. She wondered what the poetry would be like.

"Aha, I have it!" said Uncle Rand, sitting up straight and smiling. "How will this do, Honey Bunch?"

And looking at Honey Bunch with twinkling eyes, Uncle Rand said this:

"I do not mind my thumb at all,
I might have burned my pointer tall."

"Will Mrs. Miller like that?" asked Honey Bunch.

"Oh, my, yes," replied Uncle Rand. "She'll be so glad to be reminded that she didn't burn her pointer finger that she'll forget her thumb. The pointer finger, you know, Honey Bunch, is a very important finger. You can't point out things to people if you burn that finger."

"Mother won't let me point, anyway," answered Honey Bunch. "But maybe Mrs.

Miller's mother doesn't mind. Anyway, I'll
tell Mother and she will write it down for me
to send to Mrs. Miller. It makes me feel nice
to say it, Uncle Rand."

Uncle Rand's eyes were twinkling more
than ever and Honey Bunch wondered if he
could be laughing at her. She didn't mind,
because when Uncle Rand laughed you always felt like laughing, too.

"Here is Stub at last," said Uncle Rand, as
that small girl, in a spandy clean dress came
running in. "I'll write down the rhyme for
you, Honey Bunch, so run away and don't
bother your head over burned thumbs.
Where are you going?"

"Down to the pasture," called Stub, as she
took Honey Bunch's hand and pulled her
after her.

Honey Bunch told her cousin about Mrs.
Miller as they ran and the verse Uncle Rand
had made up for her, and Stub, who was used
to her daddy's rhymes, shouted:

"I do not mind my thumb at all, I might
have burned my pointer tall," all the way to

the pasture. The cows looked surprised at
her, but Stub didn't care.

"Won't they bite?" asked Honey Bunch,
when they reached the pasture gate.

There were eight or nine cows standing in
the pasture, enjoying the soft grass and gently
switching their tails as they ate. Honey
Bunch did not feel that she was exactly ac-
quainted with so many cows.

"No, of course they won't bite," answered
Stub. "Come on, we can wiggle through the
gate. It's too heavy to lift down."

Honey Bunch watched Stub crawl through
the bars and then she followed her.

"Why do they keep looking at us?" she
asked Stub, as the cows stopped eating and
stared at the two little girls.

"Oh, I suppose they want to see who we
are," answered Stub. "Let's go down by the
brook. Aunt Edith likes wild flowers so
much. Perhaps we can find some for her."

Honey Bunch knew that her mother loved
wild flowers dearly and she was eager to pick
a bouquet for her. Still, she couldn't help

wishing that the cows would go on eating grass and not look at them.

"Don't you fall into the water," said Stub. "I'm going down to the edge to look for flowers, but you'd better be careful."

Stub felt that she ought to take great care of Honey Bunch, not only because she was her visitor, but because she was a whole year younger.

Honey Bunch did not want to fall into the water, so she let Stub go ahead and the next time she looked up, there stood a cow directly in her path.

"It looked as big as—as big as—a mountain!" Honey Bunch told Liny that afternoon.

Of course the cow was no larger than any ordinary cow, but when you are only five years old an ordinary cow looks pretty tall if it is close beside you.

"Stub!" screamed Honey Bunch. "Stub, come get the cow!"

Honey Bunch was sure her cousin would not be afraid of a cow. Stub, she knew, was a brave little girl. Sure enough, she scrambled

up the bank and dashed toward the cow the
moment she heard Honey Bunch call.

"Go away, Daisy!" cried Stub. "Aren't
you ashamed of yourself?"

But Daisy stood quietly and Stub explained
that she wanted to be petted.

"Mother and Liny always pet her," explained Stub. "Daisy gives more milk than
any other cow we have. Scratch her nose,
Honey Bunch, and tell her she is nice, and
then she will walk away."

Honey Bunch put out her little hand and
scratched Daisy's nose, and Stub did, too.

"You are a very nice cow," said Honey
Bunch politely. "I like the rich milk you
give me to drink. Please, will you go away
now?"

And after Stub had patted her and told her
she was a nice cow, Daisy did turn and walk
away.

"My, Stub, how brave you are!" said
Honey Bunch, trotting along beside her
cousin. "You're not afraid of anything, are
you?"

"Well, no, hardly anything," answered Stub. "Of course, Honey Bunch, I live in the country and I'm used to cows. But I don't believe anything can really scare me."

And just as she said that, Stub shouted "Ow!" and jumped up into the air so high that Honey Bunch was frightened nearly out of her wits.

"Stub!" she cried. "Oh, Stub, what is it? Did you step on a pin?"

"I saw a snake!" gasped Stub. "A horrid snake! Right over there in the grass! Come on, let's go home."

"But we haven't got the flowers for Mother," said Honey Bunch. "And there are lots of them down there by the water—blue ones. Snakes won't bite, will they, Stub?"

Now Stub was really a sensible little girl. She knew why she was afraid, and that is more than some grown-up people can explain.

"No, none of the snakes we have around here bite," she said to Honey Bunch. "Daddy and Michael both know and they say there are none but harmless water snakes about. I

jump when I see even a tiny snake, because I
don't like them; they make me shiver, Honey
Bunch."

"Well, if they don't bite, I don't care," answered Honey Bunch. "Snakes won't make
me shiver, and I want some blue flowers for
Mother. Where was that snake you saw,
Stub? I'll chase it and then you can come
and pick flowers, too."

Stub looked at Honey Bunch in surprise.
Here was a girl who was afraid of cows and
who was not afraid of snakes. Stub liked
cows and she did not like snakes.

"It was right over there," she said, pointing
to a patch of long grass. "I saw it, just as
plain. But don't go near it, Honey Bunch.
We can walk the other way."

"I'll chase it," said Honey Bunch. "I
would like to see a snake run."

She tiptoed over to the patch of grass and
looked around carefully.

"Oh, ho, you funny Stub!" she called.
"Look!" And she stooped down and picked
up something long and dark that dangled.

"It's only rope!" cried Honey Bunch. "Just an old piece of rope! It never was a snake."

Well, of course, it never was a snake. Even Stub could see that, though she had been so sure. She laughed good-naturedly and then she and Honey Bunch picked the little blue flowers—they were violets—till they each had a nice, large bunch to take home.

"Something splashed me," said Honey Bunch, tying her bunch with a grass stem, as Stub showed her.

"It's raining," declared Stub. "We'll have to run if we don't want to get wet. It hasn't rained since you've been here, has it, Honey Bunch?"

Liny said the same thing and so did Michael. Honey Bunch and Stub found them both on the back porch. Liny was peeling potatoes for dinner and Michael was storing little new plants under the porch out of the wet. He said that he would set them out in the garden after supper that night.

"I think the rain has been holding off till

you had a chance to see the farm, Honey
Bunch," said Liny. "And now it has to make
up for the delay."

"I would rather," said Honey Bunch, "not
have it rain. I like to play outdoors with
Stub."

"My garden needs rain," Michael told her,
smilingly. "All the thirsty vegetables will get
a cool drink."

"And we can play in the barn, Honey
Bunch," said Stub. "I'll show you how to
slide down the hay. You need to practice
that."

It was raining hard by dinner time, and
after dinner Aunt Carol brought out two old
water-proof capes and gave them to Honey
Bunch and Stub.

"Now run between the drops and have a
grand time in the barn," she said, kissing each
little girl.

"That's what Mr. Popover said—to run between the drops," called Honey Bunch, as she
and Stub raced out to the big, dry barn.

Stub had heard all about Mr. and Mrs.

Popover and she thought they must be very nice indeed.

"Let's do something exciting," suggested Stub, when they had climbed into the hay-mow. "Oh, there's Buffy—he followed us out. We can bring him up here and play with him."

Buffy wasn't a very young dog and he was fat. He didn't know how to climb a ladder and he didn't care much about learning. But Stub was determined to get him into the hay-mow, and she pushed him and Honey Bunch pulled him, and, with much work and tugging, they finally managed to haul the poor dog up the ladder into the mow.

"Now we can play," said Stub, trying not to see where she had stepped on her dress and pulled a big piece out of the hem.

CHAPTER X

ONE RAINY AFTERNOON

Buffy didn't like it up in the haymow at all. He didn't feel comfortable, for one thing, and for another, he was too warm. He wore a shaggy fur coat, you see, while Honey Bunch and Stub wore gingham dresses. And besides, Buffy knew that the haymow was no place for a dog.

"We'll play he is a bear," said Stub. "Let's bury Buffy in the hay and then go hunting for him."

They heaped the hay up over the poor dog and then went burrowing like two small rabbits through the sweet, dried grass, hunting the "bear." When they found Buffy they pounced on him and told him he was captured.

"I think Buffy is tired," said Honey Bunch

at last. "I'm tired, too. Can't we sit down a minute?"

"Of course," answered Stub. "We can slide down the hay and that will rest you."

Stub never wanted to sit down and rest herself. Her daddy said that the only time she was quiet was when she was asleep.

"I'll fix the hay—you wait," she said.

So while Honey Bunch and Buffy sat down, Stub built a long hay slide on one side of the mow, pulling out the hay in one place and piling it up in another, "like a waterfall," she explained.

"Come on and slide!" she called to Honey Bunch, when it was ready.

Honey Bunch thought sliding down the hay was the most fun she had ever had.

"Look out—here I go!" shouted Honey Bunch, her cheeks as red as fire.

Down she shot. Bump! she landed on the smooth spot where Stub had pulled away the hay.

"Ouch!" cried Honey Bunch, as all the rest of the hay slid down on top of her.

There was hay in her eyes and hay in her
hair and hay sticking right into her hands and
arms—Honey Bunch could feel it. There
was a good deal of dust flying about, too, and
when Stub pulled her out, Honey Bunch was
sneezing and coughing.

"Honey Bunch!" they heard Stub's daddy
calling. "Stub! Children, where are you?"

"We'll go down," said Stub. "You won't
sneeze outdoors. Here—I'll help you down
the ladder."

Honey Bunch and Stub went carefully
down the ladder and neither one saw the
shaggy head and two brown eyes that peered
at them over the edge of the mow. They didn't
even hear Buffy when he whined.

"It's stopped raining!" said Honey Bunch,
in great surprise.

They found Uncle Rand and Michael
standing in the barn doorway. Michael was
holding one of the farm horses, "Thomas
Foote," by the bridle. When Honey Bunch
first heard that this was the horse's name, she
thought Stub must be teasing her.

"That's his name, it really is," insisted Stub.
"Michael named him, and we all call him
T. F. Michael named him so he could write
down in the blacksmith's book 'shoes for T.
Foote.' Michael said lots of people sign their
names that way and he didn't see why a horse
shouldn't have a sensible name like a man."

Honey Bunch called the horse T. Foote
after that, and Michael said it showed what
good sense she had.

"Well, what have you been doing?" asked
Uncle Rand, as soon as he saw the two little
girls. "Why, you look as though you might
have been sleeping in the haymow for a
week."

"We were playing," said Honey Bunch.

"The slide fell down on her," explained
Stub. "There's a little hay left in her hair
yet."

"A little?" repeated Uncle Rand, his eyes
twinkling. "Why, Stub, I was wondering if
there was any hay left in the mow. How can
I take the pictures of two such odd looking
people?"

Stub clapped her hands and danced about.

"Michael went to town and brought back films!" she cried. "You did, didn't you, Michael? And now Daddy can take our pictures."

But Uncle Rand said that he couldn't take their pictures while they looked as they did. They must brush their hair and shake the hay seed out. He helped them, and in a few minutes both Honey Bunch and Stub looked much better.

"The sun will be out stronger, if we wait a few minutes," said Uncle Rand. "We'll give Honey Bunch a little ride on T. Foote first."

"He's pretty far from the ground," Honey Bunch said, looking up at the gray horse who *was* pretty tall.

"All the better for you," declared Michael cheerfully. "You'll be so far above the mud you can't be splashed. Shall I lift you up?"

Honey Bunch nodded. She held her breath while Michael lifted her up and put her on the blanket folded over T. Foote's broad back. When he felt her there, the horse turned around and looked to see who was riding him.

"You look ahead, T. Foote," said Honey Bunch sternly. "My daddy says to watch the road when you're going anywhere."

Michael laughed and took the bridle, while Uncle Rand walked beside Honey Bunch and held her on with one hand. Stub danced ahead to open the barnyard gate, for Michael said it was drier in the orchard than in the yard.

"He—he rocks," gasped Honey Bunch, holding on to the thick gray mane with both hands. "But he is a very nice horse," she added quickly.

T. Foote lifted his feet very carefully and put them down softly. Honey Bunch thought he didn't want to splash her with mud, and that may have been the reason. Horses are very wise, you know, and they can understand our kind of talk much better than we understand theirs.

There was a wide path, almost as wide as a road, around the orchard, where no trees were planted. It was around this path that Michael

led T. Foote with Honey Bunch on his back.
Just as they reached the first pear tree, the sun
came out from behind the clouds, hot and
clear.

"Take her picture!" begged Stub. "Take
it now, Daddy!"

"All right, I will," said Uncle Rand.
"Michael, you come around on this side and
hold her steady. You won't show behind the
horse. Look at the camera, Honey Bunch,
please."

Honey Bunch sat up straight and held the
lines as she had seen her uncle and Michael
drive. She smiled right into the small black
box Uncle Rand carried, and when it
went click! she knew her picture had been
taken.

"Now take Stub, too," said Honey Bunch.
"I want to show Ida Camp Stub's picture."

Michael lifted Stub up on the horse, too,
and Uncle Rand took another picture. He
promised Honey Bunch she should have six to
send to her friends in Barham.

"I'll send one to Mrs. Miller," decided

Honey Bunch. "She never saw me riding on a tall horse."

As Uncle Rand turned the key again, Honey Bunch remembered Liny and the lost picture.

"If Liny's brothers were here, you could take their pictures, Uncle Rand," she said. "Walter and George, you know, who fell off the sun and moon clock."

"You always say that," laughed Stub. "How could they fall off the sun and moon clock?"

"I don't know, but they did," declared Honey Bunch. "I know I put the picture on top of the clock. And Uncle Rand would take more pictures of them for Liny, wouldn't you, Uncle Rand?"

"If Walter and George were here, I certainly should," said Uncle Rand. "But, sweetheart, if they were here, Liny wouldn't be so anxious for a picture. It is because that one was all she had and they are so many thousands of miles away from her that she feels so bad."

Every one at Broad Acres felt sorry for Liny. She thought so much of her brothers' photograph and it did seem odd that it could be lost.

"Pictures don't walk out of houses—at least I never knew them to before," Liny had said.

"Climb into the tree and I'll take a photograph of you there, Honey Bunch," said her uncle. "Don't worry your little head over Liny's picture. If it is lost, it is lost and we can't bring it back to her."

Uncle Rand took a picture of Honey Bunch in the apple tree and a picture of Stub standing on the fence, then he took a picture of them both holding out an apple for T. Foote to eat. Honey Bunch didn't hold the apple very near his mouth, but Stub knew how to hold her hand out flat and T. Foote ate her apple up so fast Honey Bunch was sure there wouldn't be any of it left to show in the picture.

"Now I'm going to drive over to Elmville," said Uncle Rand, when he had used up his roll of films. "I'll take you both, if you will run up to the house and ask the two mothers. Come, Michael, you help me harness up."

Stub's mother and Honey Bunch's mother were quite willing that their little girls should go to town with Uncle Rand. Michael harnessed T. Foote to the buggy and in a few minutes they were off.

Honey Bunch loved to drive to town. Sometimes she drove and sometimes Stub held the reins, but when they saw an automobile coming, Uncle Rand always drove. T. Foote wasn't exactly afraid of automobiles, but he liked horses better. At least that is what Stub said.

"Stub," said her daddy as they drove into town, "do you know where they sell ice-cream cones here?"

Of course Stub knew, and she and Honey Bunch went into a store and bought two chocolate ice-cream cones while Uncle Rand went to the post-office and left the pictures he had just taken at the drug store to be developed and printed. He had several other errands to do, and when they reached home again it was nearly supper time. Honey Bunch and Stub planned to play a game of croquet after supper, if they could do it before it should be half-past seven and time for bed.

They hurried out to the side lawn as soon as they had finished their meal, and they were choosing their mallets when Michael came up to them.

"Come out to the barn a moment," he said. "I want to show you something."

"We want to play a game before we have to go to bed," Stub told him. "Is it something nice, Michael?"

"It is something important," replied Michael, and that made both children curious. They could not guess what Michael wanted to show them in the barn.

He led them through the big door on to the main floor of the barn. It was still light outside, but almost as dark as night in the dim, shadowy space. Michael walked over to the haymow and Honey Bunch and Stub followed him.

"Oh, my!" gasped Stub, remembering something. "We left Buffy up there."

Buffy leaned over the mow and looked at his little mistress reproachfully. He whined.

"How could you forget me?" he seemed to be saying.

"He hasn't had a drink of water all the afternoon," said Michael. "He has not had a bite of supper. I happened to hear him when I came in to close the window in the harness room, or he might have been forgotten all night."

"I'm awfully sorry, Michael," said Stub. "It's all my fault. I didn't mean to forget Buffy—you know I didn't. He was playing with us when Daddy called us to have our pictures taken."

"Well, I'd hate to be Buffy, that's all," was Michael's reply, as he climbed up the ladder to bring poor Buffy down.

CHAPTER XI

HELPING LINY

HONEY BUNCH and Stub were very glad when Michael had helped Buffy down the ladder, and they took the dog into Liny's kitchen and fed him his favorite supper of bread and gravy with a beef bone for dessert. After that Stub, at least, was more thoughtful of her pet and tried not to leave him in places where he couldn't be comfortable.

"Honey Bunch," said Stub, one day not long after the pictures were taken—and by the way, every picture Uncle Rand took came out well and Honey Bunch sent three to her daddy and two to Ida Camp and one to Mrs. Miller—"Honey Bunch," said Stub, "I have to take this pattern over to Mrs. Phillips for mother. Don't you want to come?"

Of course Honey Bunch wanted to go with her cousin, and as soon as Stub's mother had put the pattern into a white envelope and fastened it so Stub couldn't lose it, they started. Mrs. Phillips lived next door to Broad Acres. But next door, in the country, may be rather far away, as Honey Bunch found out.

"Let's go down along the potato field," suggested Stub. "Michael is dusting the plants. Perhaps he'll whittle us a boat."

Michael had promised to make them each a boat "some day," and Stub was always reminding him.

"Michael is very neat, isn't he?" said Honey Bunch, trudging along beside Stub and trying not to step on the ants that *would* crawl in the dirt and never look to see who might be coming.

"Yes, of course he is," replied Stub. "Liny says he is the neatest hired man we ever had. She likes him. She makes the kind of dessert he likes too, and she says he never forgets to wipe his feet on rainy days before he comes into the kitchen."

"Does he use an oiled cloth?" asked Honey

Bunch, crawling under a fence after Stub, who was making a short cut across the pasture. Stub never followed a road or a path if she could help it.

"Michael use an oiled cloth, you mean?" said Stub, puzzled. "What for?"

"My mother says a feather duster isn't any good," answered Honey Bunch. "She never lets Mrs. Miller use one. She says it scatters the dust all over a room."

Stub stared at her little cousin.

"I don't know what you're talking about," she said. "Who said anything about feather dusters?"   .

"There's Michael waving to us now," Honey Bunch replied. "Nobody said anything about feather dusters, but you said Michael was dusting the plants and I just wondered how he did it."

Stub's eyes crinkled with laughter. She shouted so loudly that Michael heard her.

"Oh, Honey Bunch!" laughed Stub. "I think you are the funniest girl I ever knew! Wait till I tell Michael!"

And though Honey Bunch begged her to wait and asked her not to tell Michael, Stub began to run. She could run faster than Honey Bunch and she reached Michael first.

"Oh, Michael!" shouted Stub. "Listen to what Honey Bunch said! She said—she said ——" and then Stub was so out of breath from running and laughing that she couldn't say another word!

"Here, here, what's all the excitement about?" asked Michael, as Honey Bunch came running after Stub. "Your faces are as red as peonies. Take your time, children. I have all the morning, and so have you."

"Honey Bunch is so funny!" said Stub.

"I am not!" cried Honey Bunch. "I didn't know—that's all."

Michael stooped down and lifted Honey Bunch up and sat her on one of the fence posts. Michael wore his overalls and they and the canvas gloves that covered his hands were white with powder.

"Honey Bunch, is Stub teasing you?" he asked.

"I told her you were dusting the potato plants, and she asked me if you used an oiled cloth or a feather duster, Michael!" squealed Stub. "She thought you went around and dusted every plant the way Liny does the chairs and the tables. I never knew such a funny girl!"

Michael looked at Honey Bunch. She felt the least bit like crying, and, in fact, she had tears in her blue eyes. No one likes to be made fun of, and Stub was making fun of her, Honey Bunch was sure.

But Michael looked at her, and his eyes were so smiling and his smile began to grow and spread and in a minute Honey Bunch found herself laughing, too.

"That's much better," said Michael, patting her shoulder. "Always laugh when you want to cry and you've no idea how much better it will make you feel. Stub doesn't do any dusting at all, so she shouldn't tease you. I'm surprised at you, Stub, I really am."

Stub looked uncomfortable. She was supposed to help her mother a half hour every

Saturday morning, but she usually teased to
be allowed to go out and play and seldom did
her task, which was to dust the furniture in
the living room. So Michael knew she would
understand what he meant.

"Now I'll show you how I dust the potato
plants, Honey Bunch," he said pleasantly.
"Then you'll be able to tell Bobby and Tess
when—well some day when you see them."

Michael showed Honey Bunch how he
dusted the white powder on every plant to
keep the potato bug from eating the leaves.
Honey Bunch thought it was a lot of work, to
get the powder on each plant, and Michael
said it was.

"But when we have a large crop of potatoes
ready to dig, we forget the work," he said
cheerfully.

"Mother wants us to hurry," Stub whispered to Honey Bunch, and as she said that,
poor Stub fell over Michael's hoe which was
lying on the ground.

Michael picked her up and loaned her his
clean handkerchief. Stub needed a handker-

chief because she had been crying just a little, and that was the reason she didn't see the hoe.

"Everything's all right, Stub," Michael told her. "I know you didn't mean to make Honey Bunch cry, either. Now run along, both of you, or that pattern will be out of style before you get it to Mrs. Phillips."

This made both little girls laugh, and they ran almost all the rest of the way to the Phillips' farm. They half hoped to see the two boys who had eaten the green apples—Honey Bunch especially was anxious to ask them if they had "doubled up"—but Mrs. Phillips said they had gone to the old mill with the hired man.

"Daddy is going to drive us there some day," Stub told Honey Bunch, as they walked home. "Every week he says 'pretty soon.' There is a water wheel and it goes around and around, and it's lots of fun to hear it splash."

When they reached home they found the two mothers very busy. They were getting out clean sheets and dusting upstairs and putting fresh flowers into the vases.

"Is company coming?" asked Stub, who saw the door of the guest room open.

"Little girls should not ask questions," said her mother, smiling. "Liny is making butter this morning, dear—don't you want to take Honey Bunch out in the milk room and let her taste buttermilk?"

Honey Bunch had never seen Liny make butter. She did not churn every day, and though she had made butter several times since Honey Bunch and her mother had come to the farm, she had happened to do it on mornings when Honey Bunch was busy somewhere else.

"Hello!" said Liny, smiling, when she saw two little faces peeping in at her through the milk-room door. "Come in—the butter is almost here."

And Liny lifted the cover of the churn and let Honey Bunch look in.

"Where is the butter?" asked Honey Bunch, in surprise.

"That faint yellow patch you see will be butter soon," answered Liny. "Here, shake

the dasher a minute; then you can say you
helped to make butter."

Honey Bunch dashed the wooden stick up
and down a few times and then Liny took it
and made it go faster. She lifted the lid again
and there were golden lumps of butter, just
the kind of butter that Honey Bunch ate on
her bread.

"Is it all done?" asked Honey Bunch, staring into the churn.

"Dear, no," answered Liny. "I have to
take it out and work it and salt it before it is
ready to use. Taste this, Honey Bunch—it is
buttermilk."

Honey Bunch did not like buttermilk at all.
It tasted sour to her.

"Lots of people can't drink it," said Liny,
taking a glass for herself. "Stub won't touch
it. But Michael can drink a whole pitcherful
for his dinner."

"Are we going to have whipped cream for
dinner?" asked Stub, who had found a bowl
of sweet cream on the table.

She knew it was sweet, for she had put her

"I'VE FOUND ONE!" CALLED HONEY BUNCH.

Honey Bunch : Her First Days on the Farm.   *Page* 131

finger into it and tasted it when Liny was not
looking.

"Don't touch that," said Liny, busily scoop-
ing her butter out of the churn. "That is for
supper. But I haven't an egg in the house.
Your daddy took the basket with him to town
this morning, and now your mother wants two
cakes made. Can't you and Honey Bunch go
out and hunt me some eggs?"

Stub and Honey Bunch were sure they
could and they ran off toward the barn.
Liny's hens were supposed to lay their eggs in
the hen-house, but there were always three or
four hens who insisted on laying their eggs in
the barn. Honey Bunch and Stub thought it
was much more fun to hunt in the hay for eggs
than to go through the hen-house and pick
them out of the nests.

"You begin on that side and I'll start here,"
said Stub, pointing to the side of the barn under the haymow.

"I've found one!" called Honey Bunch in
a few moments.

"So have I!" shouted Stub.

And presently Honey Bunch found another
and so did Stub, and it wasn't long before they
had each found three eggs.

"You wait here, and I'll climb up and look
in the haymow," said Stub, running up the
ladder like a little squirrel.

"Look out—you dropped an egg!" cried
Honey Bunch, as one slipped from the skirt
of Stub's dress and smashed on the barn floor.

"Well, that's only one egg," replied Stub
cheerfully. "I can find another."

The shaky ladder began to sway, Stub
threw out both hands, and down went the
other two eggs and broke into bits on the floor.

"Silly old eggs!" scolded Stub, as though
the eggs were to blame. "Maybe I'll find
three in the haymow to make up for them."

But although she hunted a long time and
Honey Bunch waited patiently, not an egg
could Stub find.

"You can have mine," said Honey Bunch,
when Stub had climbed down again.

"No, you keep them," replied Stub.
"There'll be some more in the hen-house.

You put your eggs down on the floor and come and help me look under the heavy wagon. If there aren't any there, we'll go to the hen-house and hunt."

Honey Bunch put her three eggs down carefully, close together, and covered them with a wisp of hay. Then she and Stub crawled under the heavy wagon. Sometimes the hens would go under that and make a nest in the hay and lay their eggs.

As Honey Bunch and Stub were feeling about in the hay and, at the same time, pretending they were swimming in the ocean, they heard the rattle of wheels and T. Foote whirled the buggy in through the open barn door.

"Anybody home?" called Uncle Rand loudly.

"Look out for the eggs!" shouted Stub, wriggling out, flat on her stomach. After her wriggled Honey Bunch, crying:

"Did he step on the eggs? Did he step on the eggs?"

And there in the buggy, one on each side of

Uncle Rand, sat Bobby and Tess Turner, the twins from New York!

"Daddy," said Stub seriously, "T. Foote has stepped on the eggs Honey Bunch was saving. Hello, Tess! Bobby, can you play croquet?"

CHAPTER XII

THE OLD MILL

HONEY BUNCH was so surprised to see Bobby and Tess that she forgot about the eggs. "Mother is coming on the next train," cried Tess, jumping down and kissing both her cousins. "Bobby and I came all alone and Uncle Rand met us at the station. Didn't you know we were coming?"

"We kept the good news for a surprise," said Uncle Rand, smiling, while Bobby took a flying leap from the buggy that landed him in the hay in front of T. Foote's stall.

"Well, that's the reason Liny has to make two cakes," said Stub. "And she has to have the eggs to make 'em with. Honey Bunch and I want to look in the hen-house. You can come if you want to, Bobby and Tess."

"But Tess has her best dress on," said Honey Bunch.

"I'll be careful," promised Tess, and the four children went to hunt for eggs in the hen-house.

Stub made Bobby and Tess stand outside because, as she told them, if an egg did break it would be sure to spatter on Tess's dress or over Bobby's clean blouse.

"And eggs," said Stub, with a sigh, "mostly break when I'm trying to be careful."

She and Honey Bunch found a dozen eggs and carried them out. Stub let Bobby carry three and Tess three and those twelve eggs reached Liny's kitchen safely. Yes, and they were made into two beautiful cakes not long after that—and broken eggs are safest in a cake, you know.

The Turner twins' mother—who was "Aunt Julia" to Honey Bunch and Stub—came on the next train, and Uncle Rand declared he did not know who laughed and chattered more—the three mothers on the front porch or the four children playing croquet after supper.

It was the very next morning that Uncle Rand suggested a trip to the old mill.

"Stub has been teasing me to take Honey Bunch there for the last two weeks," said this kind uncle. "But I knew if the twins came they would want to go, too, so it seemed wiser to wait till I could make one trip."

The buggy wouldn't hold four lively children, of course, and Michael said he thought they would have to go in the "dill-do."

"What is a dill-do?" asked Honey Bunch.

"What is a dill-do, Michael?" asked Bobby and Tess in one breath.

Michael laughed and whittled the hoe handle he was fitting into a sharp, new shining hoe.

"A dill-do," he said merrily, "is a wagon."

And that must have been the right answer, for when Uncle Rand drove T. Foote out of the yard and tied him to the white hitching post that stood in front of the house, the horse was harnessed to the wagon that was used for taking the milk cans to the creamery every morning. There were two seats in it now though. As a rule, there was only one, for the driver.

Uncle Rand was to drive, and when he came out of the house he found all four youngsters sitting on the front seat waiting for him.

"No one is going to take a chance on being left, that's certain," said Uncle Rand. "But how do you expect me to drive?"

"Well, Daddy," replied Stub, "I said there wasn't room for every one up here, but no one wants to sit in the back. We all want to ride on the front seat."

"Can't be done," said Uncle Rand, standing by the post and making no move to untie T. Foote. "Two will have to go on the back seat. I must have elbow room, you know."

Bobby and Tess sat still and so did Stub. But Honey Bunch stood up.

"I'll sit in the back," she said. "I guess I almost want to, anyway."

"That's my sweet girl!" said Uncle Rand, lifting her over the back of the seat and putting her down on the second seat with a kiss. "There wouldn't be any quarrels if every one could be a Honey Bunch."

"Well, I'll go back, too," said Stub, scrambling over. "I'm used to riding in front and Bobby and Tess are company."

Bobby and Tess will change places with you, when we come back," her daddy promised. "Now then, T. Foote, let's show the city folks how fast we can travel over country roads."

Uncle Rand untied the horse and climbed into the wagon beside Bobby and Tess. He turned the wagon around and they started off down the winding white road that Honey Bunch was sure went clear around the world. She had never seen the end of it, or where it began, and neither had Uncle Rand. Honey Bunch knew he had not, because she had asked him.

"What is a mill for?" asked Bobby curiously.

"Well, now, what do you think a mill is for?" asked Uncle Rand, touching T. Foote's back with the whip to frighten off a fly that was trying to bite him.

"For millers, I guess," said Tess wisely.

"No," said Honey Bunch, "mills aren't for

millers.   They   eat   holes   in   clothes—my
mother says so."

"Those are moth millers," answered Uncle
Rand.   "They have nothing to do with the
kind of miller who runs a mill.   He grinds
corn into meal and wheat into flour for us to
eat, Bobby."

Stub, of course, knew about mills, but the
other children had a great many questions to
ask.

"This old mill we are going to see doesn't
grind any more," explained Uncle Rand, who
could drive and keep Bobby from falling off
the seat and catch Tess's hat for her when the
breeze nearly carried it away and still answer
questions.   "This mill used to be a busy one,
but when there was a larger one built to be
run by electric power in another town, people
gradually stopped going to the mill run by
water power.   Now it is about in ruins, with
nothing but the old wheel to remind us of the
busy place it used to be."

"People come and paint it," said Stub,

bouncing around on the seat like a small rubber ball. "They put it in pictures."

T. Foote jogged right along and all the talk and laughter in the wagon behind him did not seem to interest him in the least. He never stopped once to listen and he did not turn around to see what was going on. He simply kept going and that, of course, brought him to the old mill as quickly as it was possible for a good horse to get there.

"Isn't it pretty!" cried Honey Bunch, as her uncle lifted her down.

It was pretty, this old mill, and even Bobby, who liked to explore first and look afterward, stopped for a moment to see the old wheel. The mill itself had been built of stone and the stones were crumbled and broken now. There was no roof and only one side of a wall and you could see directly into the large room where the miller had worked when he ground the wheat and the corn the farmers brought him.

"The wheel is on the other side," said Stub,

catching hold of Honey Bunch by the hand.
"Come around and look."

They heard the sound of rushing water as
soon as they went close to the mill. The old
wheel was not turning, but the water went
through it and fell with a splash into a narrow
walled space below that Uncle Rand told
them had been the sluice.

"You see," he explained, holding Honey
Bunch up so that she could look into the
wheel, "when the mill was grinding, the water
struck the wheel and forced it to turn and that
turned the great stone grinders inside the mill
and the corn and wheat was crushed to powder between them."

Uncle Rand held each child up to look,
even Bobby who wanted to climb up on the
wheel and see for himself just how water
wheels were made.

"No, sir!" said Uncle Rand, when Bobby
suggested this. "Nothing like that. Your
mother made me promise that I would keep
you a good two feet from the water before she
was willing to have you come. There is

plenty to be seen without going swimming in
the sluice, Bobby."

So Bobby had to be contented with climbing all over the heaps of stones that had once
been walls and peering into the dark corners
where little green ferns were growing in place
of the big bags of grain that had once stood
there.

The floor of the mill was not safe to walk
on, and after Uncle Rand had led them
around the edge and told them more about the
big stones that had ground the corn—these
stones, he said, had been sold and carried off
when the miller closed his mill—he made
them promise that they would not go inside
the mill again.

"Hello, Morton! What brings you over
this way?" cried a jolly-looking fat man, stopping his horse in the road.

Uncle Rand went down to talk to him and
that left the twins and Honey Bunch and Stub
to amuse themselves.

"It would be fun to cross the brook," said
Stub. "Let's get a board and make a bridge."

"Uncle Rand said not to go in the mill," Honey Bunch reminded her.

"Well, I'm not going in the mill," retorted Stub. "Here's a board. Help me carry this, Bobby."

Stub pointed to an old board that lay in the grass at her feet. It was heavy, and Bobby had all he could do to help her drag it down to the brook. Stub was careful to go on the other side of the mill from the road and she knew enough to go down below the sluice. Stub was a careful little girl, and she had no intention of getting drowned. The water in the sluice was deep enough to drown a boy or a girl, but the brook was not deep.

"Come on," cried Stub. "Come on, Tess and Honey Bunch. We're going to have a heap of fun!"

Honey Bunch and Tess followed Stub and Bobby who were almost out of breath when they reached the brook. The board was much heavier than Stub had thought it would be, but she did not give up easily.

"It won't reach," said Bobby, after he had

put the board down. "It isn't long enough."

"Well, put it across as far as it will go," replied Stub impatiently. "Then we can hop the rest of the way on the stones."

Bobby dragged the board to the edge of the brook and let it fall so that one end rested on a large stone. The other was on the bank.

"There!" said Stub. "That's a bridge. I'll go over first."

Stub's dress was torn, because there had been a nail in the board. Stub's hands and face were streaked with dirt, for the board had been old and dusty. But Stub was having a very good time—Honey Bunch knew it by the way she smiled.

"Here I go!" sang Stub, running down and out on her bridge. "Watch me!"

They all watched her, but Stub was so afraid they might miss seeing something she did that she turned her head and looked back over her shoulder to make sure they were looking.

Alas! Stub's toe hit a knot-hole in the

board, she tripped, lost her balance and fell screaming into the water!

"Uncle Rand!" shouted Honey Bunch. "Uncle Rand, come quick! Stub fell in the brook! Stub fell in the brook!"

Uncle Rand came flying around the mill and the fat man came running after him, but Bobby waded into the brook without waiting for them. The water was not deep, but it was cold, and Stub had tumbled in flat on her face. Bobby pulled her up, but before he could drag her to her feet Uncle Rand had come stepping over the stones and had her in his arms.

"Are you hurt, dear?" he said, holding her tightly. "Don't be frightened—Daddy has you safe, Stub."

Stub could not get her breath at first, but when she could speak she opened her mouth as widely as she could and how she roared! Honey Bunch stared at her, and Bobby began to laugh.

CHAPTER XIII

SUNDAY SCHOOL

"I'M co-old!" roared Stub. "I'm so co-old! I want to go ho-ome!"

"Here, you, stop laughing," said the fat man to Bobby. "You wouldn't think it was funny if you had fallen head-first into that cold water. Run up to the wagon and get the blankets out from under the seat."

"All right, I w-will!" stuttered Bobby, his teeth chattering. "It is c-cold, isn't it?"

Bobby had been in the water, too, you see, and though he was not as wet as Stub, still he was beginning to shake and shiver as she did.

"We'll get the blankets!" said Honey Bunch quickly. "Hurry up, Tess. I saw them under the seat."

The two little girls ran up to the fence where the horse and wagon were tied. Sure enough, there were two heavy blankets folded

147

under the seat. Honey Bunch dragged them
out, but Stub and Uncle Rand and Bobby had
reached the wagon almost as soon as she and
Tess had and she did not have to carry them
down to the brook.

"There, there, Stub, you're all right," said
Uncle Rand, wrapping one of the blankets
around Stub. "Now let me bundle up Bobby,
and we'll be home before you can say Jack
Robinson."

Bobby was wrapped in the other blanket
and put on the back seat. Then Uncle Rand
lifted in Stub, who was still crying, and made
Honey Bunch sit next to her so that she would
not fall off the seat. Stub was so bundled up
she looked like a package more than she did
like a little girl.

Tess sat on the back seat with Bobby and T.
Foote went home with them all as fast as he
could.

"Is anything the matter?" asked Aunt
Carol, coming down the steps when the wagon
drove up and stopped. "Has anything
happened?"

Well, you may be sure when the three mothers heard what had happened there was a great scurrying to and fro. Stub and Bobby were rubbed dry and put to bed and fed hot soup and every one waited on them and tried to keep them warm and contented, because Uncle Rand said he thought they should stay in bed till supper time. And neither of them took the tiniest bit of a cold from their tumbles and they had forgotten about the cold water before breakfast the next morning.

The next day was Sunday, and Stub felt very important because she had three cousins to take to Sunday school.

"We have to go to church first," said Stub. "Sunday school is after that. Do you go to Sunday school in New York, Bobby?"

"Of course we do," said Tess, answering for Bobby. "Only we have Sunday school at half-past nine in the morning, before church begins."

Uncle Rand took them all to church in a comfortable, cushioned carriage and Honey Bunch liked the square white-painted church as soon as she saw it. She thought it would have been nicer to have the service outdoors under the weeping willow trees, and it would certainly have been cooler.

"You can go to sleep after the long prayer," whispered Stub. "It isn't wrong. It's only wrong to whisper and laugh in church."

"I won't go to sleep," whispered Bobby who had overheard. "I never go to sleep in church. I always listen."

Honey Bunch decided that she would not go to sleep, either. She liked the music and the singing and when the tall, thin minister stood up and began to preach, she sat up very straight and listened.

"Isn't it funny—" she thought to herself, "isn't it funny—how—the sun turns—red—and—green—and yellow."

Honey Bunch was looking at the stained glass window and without knowing it she went to sleep, leaning against her mother. A loud noise woke her up.

"What was that?" she said aloud.

"Hush, dear!" whispered her mother.

"Bobby went to sleep and fell off the seat. Uncle Rand has picked him up."

There were a few people who were smiling and one man in the pew ahead of them laughed outright. Bobby's face was very red, but Uncle Rand did not smile. He acted as though he was quite used to seeing people fall off their seats in church. This made Bobby feel better—he hated to be laughed at.

Honey Bunch did not go to sleep again, and after the service had ended she and Stub and Bobby and Tess went into the Sunday-school room which was back of the church.

"How do you do, Mary?" said a young lady to Stub.

Honey Bunch did not know at first that she was speaking to Stub. "Mary" sounded as though she must mean some other little girl, though, of course, that was Stub's real name.

"Miss Carter," said Stub, "these are my cousins Honey Bunch—she lives in Barham. And Bobby and Tess Turner—they live in New York."

"I am very glad to know you," said Miss

Carter. "You may sit with Mary in that
third row. Willy, stop teasing your sister, or I shall have to send you to the platform."

"Where's the platform?" whispered Honey
Bunch.

"Up there, where the man sits," Stub whispered back. "He's the superintendent. If
the boys are bad, they have to go and sit on the
edge of the platform. One Sunday there was
a row of 'em all the way round the three
sides."

There was a piano in one corner of the
room, and Miss Carter sat down at that and
played a hymn while the whole school rose
and sang. Then the superintendent read the
Scripture lesson and said the Lord's prayer
and then it was time to teach the lesson. Each
class did not have a separate room, as they did
in the twins' Sunday school. But instead each
class made a little circle around its teacher
and listened while she taught them.

"Where's Mother?" Honey Bunch whispered, as Miss Carter was giving out little

lesson books. "Did she and Aunt Carol and
Aunt Julia go home?"

"No, they're in the church," Stub explained.
"The grown-up people have Bible classes in
the church. They have to wait for us, and
they can have a class while they're waiting,
you see."

Honey Bunch listened and heard the organ
and the sound of singing. She thought it was
nice for every one to go to Sunday school at
the same time.

"Mary, will you ask your cousin to read the
first verse of our lesson?" said Miss Carter.

"Tess can read, but Honey Bunch can't,"
said Stub. "She's only five years old. Go on,
Tess."

Tess read a verse so fast that no one could
understand a word of what she was saying, but
Miss Carter did not ask her to read it again.
Perhaps she thought it would not be polite.

Stub could not read very well, but Miss
Carter helped her with the hard words, and
then a little girl, named Fannie Morgan, read
a verse. Then it was Bobby's turn, but he was

too shy. The idea of reading before so many
strange people did not suit him at all.

"I can't read," he said when Miss Carter
looked at him.

"Why, you can, too," said his sister. "Can't
he, Stub?"

"Of course he can. He's eight years old,
and any one can read when he's eight," declared Stub, as though that settled it.

"I tell you I can't read," protested Bobby.

He really meant that he couldn't read unless he felt comfortable and at home. If he
stood up in this strange place and tried to read
a verse from a strange lesson paper, he knew
his face would get red and his hands shake
and, worst of all, perhaps his voice might
sound shaky, too. And he could see that there
were ever so many long Bible names he
couldn't say.

"I think you ought to read a verse, if you
can, Bobby," said Miss Carter. "We should
take a part in Sunday school whenever we can,
you know."

"Well, I can't read—that's all," muttered

Bobby, wishing he had never come to Sunday school.

Honey Bunch felt sorry for him. She knew how she would feel if Miss Carter spoke to her like that. She knew Bobby wasn't happy, and Honey Bunch couldn't be happy herself if she saw some one else having what Mrs. Miller called a "worrying spell."

"Bobby can find places on the map, Miss Carter," explained Honey Bunch. "He can read names, but he can't say 'em."

Bobby looked at his little cousin gratefully. That was exactly what he could do. He could not pronounce the names of the old cities, but he loved to find them on the Bible maps and he and Tess had spent many a happy Sunday afternoon sticking pins in the names of the towns and cities that had been mentioned in their morning Sunday-school lesson. Honey Bunch knew Bobby liked to do this, for she had seen him do it when she visited the twins in New York.

"That is nice to know," said Miss Carter more kindly. "Suppose you take your lesson paper, Bobby, and this map and box of pins, and put a pin on every city you find mentioned in the lesson."

This pleased Bobby very much and he set to work at once, while Miss Carter went around the circle, asking each one to read a verse. By the time they had finished reading the lesson, Bobby had the map covered with black-headed pins, and when Miss Carter looked at it she said he had not missed a single town or city.

"Look at the boys," whispered Stub to Honey Bunch, as Miss Carter began to teach.

Honey Bunch looked. There on the platform sat five or six boys who had been sent from their classes because they had whispered or teased other boys or had, in some way, interfered with the lesson.

The lesson Miss Carter was teaching them this Sunday was about the heathen, and she told them all about the good missionaries who went far away to teach sick and ignorant and unhappy people who had no church and Sunday schools.

"Perhaps when you grow up, you'll be a missionary, Mary," said Miss Carter to Stub.

"Well, perhaps," said Stub, but she did not seem at all sure about it.

Afterward she told Honey Bunch that she wouldn't mind being a missionary if she could stay at home and be one.

When Sunday school was over, they found the three mothers and Uncle Rand waiting for them. Uncle Rand asked Honey Bunch what she had learned.

"About heathen," she said, waiting for him to lift her into the carriage.

"But, dear, you have your money in your hand," said her mother. "Why didn't you put it in the collection box."

Honey Bunch shook her head.

"I don't want the heathen to have it," she said seriously. "I'm saving it for the bad boys."

She meant the boys who had been sent to sit on the edge of the platform. Stub said she didn't see why Honey Bunch should want to give her money to them.

"They're not heathen," said Stub.

"Yes, I think they are heathen," laughed Uncle Rand. "Only I don't believe that is why Honey Bunch wants to give them her money. Why is it, dear? Can't you tell us? We won't laugh."

"Well, the reason is," said Honey Bunch, "I found it. They hid it under the edge of the carpet and I went and took it out."

In spite of his promise, Uncle Rand laughed.

"They thought they'd save their Sunday-school money and buy lollypops on the way home," he chuckled. "But they didn't know a little squirrel had come to Sunday school. What will you do next, Honey Bunch?"

"She must find the boys and give the money back to them," said Honey Bunch's mother. "It belongs to them."

CHAPTER XIV

SEVERAL SURPRISES

HONEY BUNCH looked at the six pennies in her hand.

"Maybe they're looking for them now," she said.

"They probably are," declared Uncle Rand. "We'll go back in the Sunday-school room and look."

The others stayed in the carriage while he and Honey Bunch went into the room back of the church. There on their hands and knees on the floor were six very uncomfortable boys, searching for something. Their Sunday-school teacher, a severe-looking woman with spectacles, stood by, holding a wooden box in her hands.

"If you put any money there, it must be there now," she said. "And if you have spent your collection money this week again, I'll tell your mothers and you'll be kept home from the picnic."

"Here's the money," said Honey Bunch.

Red and tumbled, the boys stood up. Their teacher looked surprised. She asked Honey Bunch if she were sure the money belonged to them, and Honey Bunch said she was sure.

"Then give it to them," said the teacher, "and I'll see that each one puts his penny in the box."

"Will the heathen get it?" asked Honey Bunch.

"The heathen will," replied the teacher grimly. "Though if the heathen in foreign lands are any worse than those I teach every Sunday, I'm ashamed to say I don't think the money will do them much good."

As Honey Bunch and her uncle walked back to the carriage, he asked her why she had picked up the pennies from under the carpet.

"I just wanted to make those boys surprised," said Honey Bunch, and she laughed a gay little giggle.

Uncle Rand laughed, too. He and Honey

Bunch could always see a joke, and that was the reason she thought he was so much like her daddy.

"Where's the picnic?" asked Bobby, as soon as Honey Bunch told them what the Sunday-school teacher had said.

They were driving home, and Honey Bunch stood up on the floor of the carriage to talk to Bobby and Tess, who were riding in front.

"It's the big Grange picnic," said Stub. "It's Thursday, isn't it, Mother? And we're all going. Every single person in our house."

"Are Liny and Michael going?" asked the twins, both of them.

"Yes, they always go," explained Stub. "And the picnic is in Holder's grove and we go right after breakfast and stay till milking time."

That was all the children talked about after that—the big picnic. Liny was the busiest person on the farm, or she said she was. She had chickens to dress and cook and sandwiches and cake to make and boxes to pack and her

new pink lawn dress to iron. The three mothers were busy, too, and Michael washed and
polished the buggy and the carriage till they
shone. He oiled the harness, too, and then,
the day before the picnic, he brushed and
combed T. Foote and his mate, W. Vane, because T. Foote was to take the family in the
carriage and W. Vane was to take Michael
and Liny in the buggy to the picnic.

"What does W. Vane mean?" repeated
Michael, when Honey Bunch once questioned
him. "Why, I'll tell you. That stands for
Weather Vane, because that horse is as
changeable as the weather. But we shorten
it because we don't like to hurt his feelings."

"I'm so tired I could cry," said Liny, ironing her pink lawn dress when Honey Bunch
peeped into the kitchen the afternoon before
the picnic. "I counted on Michael bringing
in the turkeys for me, and now he tells me he's
going to drive Mrs. Turner and your mother
over to town. I don't care if those turkeys
never come back. I'm not going to chase
after them."

Honey Bunch looked at Liny. She sounded
cross, and yet Liny was never cross. And the
flock of young turkeys were the pride of her
heart. Not many people raised turkeys
around Elmville, and Liny said it was because
they didn't have the patience. It took lots of
patience, she once explained to Honey Bunch.

"Turkeys can't live if you shut them up
close like chickens," said Liny. "And yet if
you let them out you have to go after them and
bring them in every time because they never
know enough to come home. And a heavy
dew will kill them if they stay out in it before
they get grown."

Honey Bunch had often seen Liny hunting
her turkeys, and now she knew there must be
something very wrong indeed if Liny didn't
care whether they never came back.

"I'll go after them for her," said Honey
Bunch to herself.

The twins had gone with Uncle Rand to
see the baby pigs on the Phillips farm, but
Honey Bunch had not cared to go with them.
She thought baby pigs were rather homely.

Stub and Aunt Carol had gone to another
neighbor's to take a loaf cake for their picnic
basket and, as Michael had driven Honey
Bunch's mother and Aunt Julia over to town,
Honey Bunch found herself alone.

"I'll go get the turkeys," she said again.

She knew that they were usually found in
one of the large grass fields, but Honey Bunch
had never been in a grass field, and when she
climbed through the bars she found the grass
was almost as high as her head.

"It's like wading in the water," she whispered, for somehow it was so still and quiet
in the big field she did not want to speak
loudly.

It was like wading, and Honey Bunch went
in deeper and deeper. Then she heard a rus-
tle and saw a bronze wing. It was a turkey.

"Liny goes all around and shoos 'em up,"
said Honey Bunch, remembering.

It was hard work, "going around" the
turkeys, for they scattered and ran through
the tall grass at every chance. Honey Bunch
did not know that Liny usually waited till a

little later in the afernoon when the turkeys
would come out of the grass to hunt for their
supper. Then she could see them easily and
drive them in with less trouble.

"It is—a—little hot!" said poor Honey
Bunch, chasing a saucy turkey who seemed to
like to go in the opposite direction.

The tall grass was hot and by the time the
little girl had shooed every turkey out and
into the pasture, her face was red from the
heat and her yellow hair was wet with per-
spiration.

Honey Bunch never thought of stopping
now she had the turkeys as far as the pasture.
From side to side she went, gently waving the
skirt of her dress as she had seen Liny wave
her apron, to drive the turkeys toward the
barnyard. Back and forth Honey Bunch
trudged, waiting patiently while the turkeys
stopped on one side of the fence, slowly
hopped down on the other side and began a
still slower march to the house.

Liny was just coming out of the kitchen,
warm and tired from her ironing, to start

after her turkeys when she saw the flock coming up the road, Honey Bunch behind them.

"I found them!" cried Honey Bunch. "Are they all there, Liny?"

"Two — four — six — twelve — sixteen —twenty—" counted Liny rapidly. "Twenty-six — thirty! Every single one, Honey Bunch, you blessed lamb! But how could you do it all yourself? And you look so tired!"

"They were kind of silly," replied Honey Bunch, dropping down on the grass under the horse-chestnut tree. "They kept going back."

Liny scattered corn in the yard and shut the big gate. She said she would shut the turkeys in the barn an hour later.

"In three more weeks they can roost outdoors," she said. "Now you come in, Honey Bunch, and I'll make you the nicest lemonade you ever tasted to pay you for all that hard work."

The next day was the picnic, and every one woke early and smiling.

Holder's grove, where the picnic was held,

was several miles from Uncle Rand's farm, and it seemed to Honey Bunch that it couldn't possibly be a large enough place to hold all the people who started for it. There were carriages and automobiles, filled with people and lunch boxes, and boys on bicycles and young men on motorcycles and some young people on horseback, all traveling the roads that lead to the grove. Liny and Michael drove away in the buggy and looked very bright and happy.

Then, when they reached the grove, there seemed to be plenty of room. There were board tables under the trees for the luncheons and swings for the children and a little brook to wade in. There were shady places for the horses to stand and a whole field for the automobiles who didn't care if the sun did pour down on their tops.

There were dozens of children, and Stub knew most of them. Such games of tag they had! Stub tripped over a pine cone and fell down, but she wasn't hurt, and though, a little later, she fell over a stone sunk in the ground,

she wasn't hurt that time either, for she fell on
a pile of soft leaves.

"Here's the tintype man!" cried one of the
boys, after lunch, pointing down the road.
"He'll take our pictures."

Uncle Rand said the four cousins must be
taken together, and that reminded Honey
Bunch again of the picture of Walter and
George, Liny's brothers, which had been so
strangely lost.

"I put it on top of the sun and moon clock,"
said Honey Bunch. "I know I did."

Bobby and Tess had not heard of the photograph, so Honey Bunch told them about it.
Bobby said a wind must have blown it out of
the kitchen and Tess was sure the vacuum
cleaner had sucked it up.

"Aunt Carol hasn't a vacuum cleaner," said
Honey Bunch. "And there wasn't a wind.
Besides, it wasn't in the kitchen. I put it in
the living-room and there was a screen in
every window."

"Well, then," said Bobby, "where did it
go?"

Honey Bunch, of course, could not tell him. The tintype man came and set up his little tent at the edge of the grove and for several hours was very busy taking pictures. He printed them and gave them to the picnic folk right there, so when it came time to go home Honey Bunch and Stub and Bobby and Tess each had a picture to put in his or her pocket.

"It was the nicest picnic," said Honey Bunch a little sleepily, at the end of the day when Uncle Rand lifted her into the seat beside him.

"Yes, wasn't it?" agreed the twins, trying not to yawn.

Playing all day in the open air has a way of making small people sleepy, you know. Stub could hardly keep her eyes open.

"I thought we left Buffy in the barn with the door closed, so he couldn't follow us," said Stub, sitting up straight as they turned into the road that led to the house. "Look, Daddy, there's Buffy on the porch."

"Perhaps Michael and Liny came home the shorter way and got here before we did," said

Stub's mother. "That certainly is Buffy on the porch, and some one is with him."

The some one stood up and waved his hat to them, and then Honey Bunch knew who it was.

"Daddy!" she shouted. "Oh, Daddy, you missed the picnic!"

Mr. Morton came down to the gate and Honey Bunch jumped into his arms almost before Uncle Rand had stopped the horse.

"Surprised you, didn't I?" Mr. Morton said, smiling. "I could get a week off if I took it at once, so I came. I found the place deserted and the dog whining for company in the barn. I knew you'd be home soon, so I waited."

"My goodness, Daddy," whispered Honey Bunch, "s'pose you hadn't!"

CHAPTER XV

WHAT THE BEES SAID

As Uncle Rand said, a week was not very long, but then it was much better than no visit at all from his brother.

"I didn't know you were Uncle Rand's brother," said Honey Bunch to her daddy one afternoon when she found them laughing in the barn while Mr. Morton tinkered with the car.

Mr. Morton had explained that they were laughing at the recollection of something that had happened when they were boys.

"Oh, Honey Bunch, you've forgotten!" said her daddy. "I've often told you how Uncle Rand and I went to school together and how I used to do his arithmetic for him and he used to draw my maps for me. Why, dear, you knew Uncle Rand was Daddy's brother. You've forgotten, that's all."

"I knew he was your brother when you were a little boy," said Honey Bunch. "But I thought it was different when folks were grown up."

Daddy Morton explained that brothers were always brothers and that Honey Bunch's mother was a sister of the Uncle Peter who came to see them every year.

"They were brother and sister when they were a little boy and girl and they always will be," said Mr. Morton. "Aunt Julia is Daddy's sister, too, you know. But don't bother your head about brothers and sisters and uncles and aunts. Let me see you slide down the hay. Stub tells me you can slide now without shutting your eyes."

Honey Bunch at first had shut her eyes tight whenever she slid down a pile of hay, but she didn't do that any more. She could slide as well as Stub and she thought, did Honey Bunch, that when she grew up she would have a farm of her own and have Michael and Liny and Buffy and Stub come and live on it with her.

"Honey Bunch," said Uncle Rand, a morning or two after Honey Bunch's daddy had come, "I don't believe you have seen my bees, have you?"

"No, she hasn't," said Aunt Carol quickly. "I have been too busy to take her, and Stub can't go near the hives. If she ever stubbed her toe and fell into one, all the poetry in the world couldn't make her feel comfortable. And now, since the twins came, I told the children they must stay away from the bee-hives. I don't honestly know what effect Bobby would have on bees," added Aunt Carol, "but I don't want to risk a visit from him to them."

Aunt Julia laughed. She said she thought it would be just as well if Bobby and Tess didn't go calling on Uncle Rand's bees.

"I want Honey Bunch to see them before she goes home," said Uncle Rand. "She is such a quiet little girl, I know they will like her. We'll go after breakfast."

Now, Honey Bunch was sure she didn't like bees. She knew they could sting, and

whenever she saw one humming around above
a pink clover flower, she always left that pink
clover flower strictly alone.

But Honey Bunch was a polite little girl,
as well as a quiet one, and she did not want
to hurt her uncle's feelings. So after breakfast she took the hand he held out to her and
they went away together to visit the bees.

Back of the house was a flower garden,
filled with the sweetest flowers Honey Bunch
had ever seen. Uncle Rand told her, as they
walked down the red brick path of this garden, that it was partly for the bees that all
the flowers were planted.

"Of course Aunt Carol couldn't be happy
without her flowers," said Uncle Rand. "But
while fields of clover and buckwheat please
the bees, they like flowers, too. They make
honey from the yellow dust you find in the
heart of a flower, and as I don't want my bees
to go too far from home, I take pains to plant
the flowers they like."

Honey Bunch pressed a little closer to her

uncle when they came to the houses where the bees lived.

"I'll wait here," she said. "They—they might not know who I am."

Uncle Rand laughed, but softly.

"I'll tell them," he answered. "Bees like quiet folk, Honey Bunch, and they're only rude and noisy when frightened or annoyed. You watch me. I'll tell the bees you are here."

Honey Bunch watched. She saw Uncle Rand walk up to one of the hives and put his hand inside. When he drew it out, there were black bees walking about on his fingers.

"Bees," said her uncle, walking carefully over to the old tree stump where Honey Bunch sat, "this is my dear little niece. She lives in Barham. Her name is Honey Bunch. And she loves sweet honey on her bread and butter in the winter time. What do you say to that?"

He bent down his head and listened.

"The bees say that they will be glad to

make sweet honey for a little girl whose name
is Honey Bunch," said Uncle Rand, smiling
at Honey Bunch, who was too interested to
smile back. "They say all the time you are
at the seashore, they'll be busy getting honey
from the flowers and storing it up for you."

"Really and truly?" asked Honey Bunch.
"Really and truly, Uncle Rand?"

"Really and truly," said her uncle. "Next
winter you may expect a comb of honey, addressed to you and sent you by the bees. You
see if you don't get it."

"Then thank you very much, dear bees,"
said Honey Bunch, standing on tiptoe to look
down at the bees walking about on Uncle
Rand's hand. "I think you are very good to
work so hard."

Uncle Rand put the bees back, and then he
and Honey Bunch walked down to the mail
box together where they found Stub and the
twins waiting for them.

"Did the bees sting you?" asked Bobby.

"No, of course not," said Honey Bunch,
who felt as though she knew the bees well

by this time. "Bees are just like other folks, Bobby."

Bobby did not think they were, but the mail carrier brought the mail just then and there was a race to see who could reach the house first.

"This letter is from Julie's mother," said Honey Bunch's mother, opening the letter her little girl brought her. "Dear, would you like to visit Julie next week?"

"At the seashore?" cried Honey Bunch. "Oh, Uncle Rand said the bees would make honey for me to eat while I was at the seashore, so he must have known. But, Mother, what will we do without Stub and Bobby and Tess and Aunt Julia and Aunt Carol and Uncle Rand and Michael and Liny?"

Everybody laughed at this long list, and Honey Bunch's mother said that perhaps Stub and the twins would visit Julie while Honey Bunch was there.

"Daddy says he will take us, before he has to make another long trip," explained Mrs. Morton. "We'll have to go home, first, but

Glenhaven isn't hard to reach and the trip
will not be too far to make in the car."

"Honey Bunch hasn't seen the ocean, but
we have," said the twins. "We've been to
the seashore lots of times."

"I'll tell Michael to hurry up and whittle
those boats," promised Stub. "If I go to see
Julie, I'll need a boat."

And that very afternoon the four children
played "seashore" in Stub's sand box which
she had under a tree and hardly ever played
in at all. What happened to Honey Bunch
at the real seashore I'll tell you in another
book, to be called, "Honey Bunch: Her First
Visit to the Seashore." She was a very little
girl to pay a visit to the very big ocean, and
she found so much to do and see that it is no
wonder it takes a whole book to tell it.

"I am so hot," declared Tess, after they had
been playing in the sand box an hour or two.
"Let's go where it is cooler."

"We'll go down cellar," suggested Stub.
Stub could always think of something to do
or somewhere to go, her daddy said. "It's

cool down there. Liny has the doors open, to air it."

The cellar doors were open and the four children walked down the short stone steps into the cool, light cellar. It was in perfect order, for Liny was as neat as a pin—Honey Bunch had heard Aunt Carol say so.

"Let's play three-cornered tag," suggested Tess, forgetting that she was warm. "I'll be it. Choose your corners."

Honey Bunch took her place behind one of the whitewashed pillars. Tess said that would count as a corner. Stub couldn't make up her mind where she wanted to go, and while she was waiting Honey Bunch looked down at the floor and saw something gray against the wall.

"It's a piece of pasteboard," she said to herself. "I wonder what's on the other side."

She stooped down and picked it up and turned it over.

"I've found it!" she shrieked, running for the stairs that led to the kitchen. "Stub! Liny! I've found it!"

The other children did not know what
Honey Bunch had found, but they ran after
her and four pairs of shoes clattered up the
stairs and four pairs of hands burst open the
kitchen door and four voices cried: "Liny!
Liny!"

No wonder Liny, who was mixing potato
salad for supper, was so surprised she dropped
the potato knife. But when she saw what
Honey Bunch had in her hand, Liny almost
smothered Honey Bunch in one big hug.

"What is it?" Stub kept asking. "What
did she find? Show us, Liny."

"It's the photograph!" cried Honey Bunch,
when she had wriggled out of Liny's arms.
"Look, Walter and George! Look, Bobby!"

The three mothers had heard the noise, and
they came to see what the matter was. When
they saw the picture, of course they asked
who had found it and where it had been
found. Every one went downstairs to look at
the spot where Honey Bunch had found it,
and Aunt Carol said it must have slipped
down behind the mantel and worked its way

down to the cellar. And that was what had happened.

"This house is so old the cracks are wide and deep," said Aunt Carol. "Well, Honey Bunch, if ever I lose anything, I shall send for you to come and find it."

"I knew I put it on top of the sun and moon clock," said Honey Bunch happily.

Liny thought that Honey Bunch was the most wonderful little girl she ever knew, because she had found the long-lost picture, and when it came time for the Mortons to start for home, Liny packed a basket of lunch that Daddy Morton said would have lasted them all the way to Japan.

"Good-by, darling," whispered Liny, standing on the step of the car to kiss Honey Bunch. "I hope you'll come to Broad Acres again very soon."

They all crowded around to say good-by, and Michael even brought out T. Foote and W. Vane and let them stand at the big gate of the barnyard to watch the car start off. The twins and Stub and Buffy had to be taken off the running boards at least a dozen times, and finally Mr. Morton had to make the start while Stub was in the middle of a sentence.

"Good-by!" they all called. "Good-by— don't forget to write."

Honey Bunch stood up and held on to her mother's hand, waving until a turn in the road hid the farmhouse from her sight."

"I feel—I feel funny," said Honey Bunch, sitting down.

"Do you know that we are going to stop and see Mr. and Mrs. Popover?" asked Mr. Morton. "Well, we are, and you'd better begin to think what you want to tell them, for they'll have many questions to ask you."

Honey Bunch began to think and she did not feel "funny" any more. So we'll leave her thinking pleasant thoughts to tell Mrs. Popover and you may remember her as a smiling little Honey Bunch.

THE END

This Isn't All!

Would you like to know what became of the good friends you have made in this book?

Would you like to read other stories continuing their adventures and experiences, or other books quite as entertaining by the same author?

On the *reverse side* of the wrapper which comes with this book, you will find a wonderful list of stories which you can buy at the same store where you got this book.

Don't throw away the Wrapper

Use it as a handy catalog of the books you want some day to have. But in case you do mislay it, write to the Publishers for a complete catalog.

THE BOBBSEY TWINS BOOKS
For Little Men and Women
By LAURA LEE HOPE
Author of "The Bunny Brown Series," Etc.

**Durably Bound. Illustrated. Uniform Style of Binding.
Every Volume Complete in Itself.**

These books for boys and girls between the ages of three and
ten stand among children and their parents of this generation
where the books of Louisa May Alcott stood in former days. The
haps and mishaps of this inimitable pair of twins, their many adventures and experiences are a source of keen delight to imaginative children.

THE BOBBSEY TWINS
THE BOBBSEY TWINS IN THE COUNTRY
THE BOBBSEY TWINS AT THE SEASHORE
THE BOBBSEY TWINS AT SCHOOL
THE BOBBSEY TWINS AT SNOW LODGE
THE BOBBSEY TWINS ON A HOUSEBOAT
THE BOBBSEY TWINS AT MEADOW BROOK
THE BOBBSEY TWINS AT HOME
THE BOBBSEY TWINS IN A GREAT CITY
THE BOBBSEY TWINS ON BLUEBERRY ISLAND
THE BOBBSEY TWINS ON THE DEEP BLUE SEA
THE BOBBSEY TWINS IN THE GREAT WEST
THE BOBBSEY TWINS AT CEDAR CAMP
THE BOBBSEY TWINS AT THE COUNTY FAIR
THE BOBBSEY TWINS CAMPING OUT
THE BOBBSEY TWINS AND BABY MAY
THE BOBBSEY TWINS KEEPING HOUSE
THE BOBBSEY TWINS AT CLOVERBANK
THE BOBBSEY TWINS AT CHERRY CORNERS
THE BOBBSEY TWINS AND THEIR SCHOOL-
    MATES
THE BOBBSEY TWINS TREASURE HUNTING
THE BOBBSEY TWINS AT SPRUCE LAKE

GROSSET & DUNLAP, Publishers, NEW YORK